Perverse

WOL-VRIEY

Burning Bulb
PUBLISHING

Other Books By Wol-vriey:

The Bizarro Story of I
Meat Suitcase
Chainsaw Cop Corpse
Vegan Zombie Apocalypse
Boston Posh (Bud Malone #1)
Vegan Vampire Vaginas
Vagina Mundi
Melanie Nemesis Catchpole
Bizarro 101: A Basic Primer
Boston Corpse (Bud Malone #2)
Dr. Orgasm
Boston Lust (Bud Malone #3)
Pussy Transmission
Hell Dancer
Girls Are Not Smiling
Brainchew
Brainchew 2: Out of Their Heads
Blue Nightmares
Daria (An Erotic Nightmare)
Wet Bones
Mr. Ugly
Brutal
Evil
666
The Cleaverman

Novellas and Short Stories By Wol-vriey

Big Trouble in Little Ass
Forever Ago Sunshine

Perverse

WOL-VRIEY

Perverse
By **Wol-vriey**

Burning Bulb Publishing
P.O. Box 4721
Bridgeport, WV 26330-4721
United States of America
www.BurningBulbPublishing.com

Cover designed by Wol-vriey and Gary Lee Vincent with photos from the following artists on Pexel.com: Isabella Mariana, Alexander Stemplewski, Luan Oosthuizen, and Elti Meshau.
Author Photo: Lolade Akinsowon © 2014.

First Edition.

Paperback Edition ISBN: 978-1-948278-22-5

Printed in the United States of America

CHAPTER 1

Heather

It was late Friday afternoon and the old green pickup truck was somewhere in northwest Massachusetts, heading up north to Searsburg in the New England state of Vermont. The vehicle and its quartet of female passengers were currently between small towns, with breathtaking mountain scenery ahead and on their left and lush woodland on their right.

Heather thought the last town they'd driven through was called Plainfield, but she wasn't sure (or was it actually Ashfield?). For most of the transit through it she'd been saying something to Katie, who was driving the pickup truck, and had only fleetingly noticed the town name on a storefront sign. Most of these small New England towns looked the same anyway: houses, vehicles, people, pets and lots of vegetation, so that each town came upon one suddenly as if it was traveling towards you instead of the reverse being the case.

There were four of them in Katie's battered Ford truck. All girls. Heather was riding shotgun beside Katie. Then there were Danni and Maude in the backseat, both of whom weren't paying the slightest attention to the coming and going countryside scenery. Which Heather found a bit odd, seeing as this trip was Danni's idea. Both of the young women in the backseat were riveted to their cellphones: Danni was on Instagram, while Maude was wearing earphones and playing a game.

Danni finally looked up from her phone. "Hey, guys, we there yet?"

"Nope," Heather replied, "Katie's still short-cutting us through life."

"Ha ha," Katie retorted from the driver's seat, slowing the Ford pickup truck a little as they rode up a hill. "Through life, indeed.

Danni, we've still got thirty minutes at least before you'll be seeing your cute boyfriend again."

"Ray's my ex, but we're still on good terms."

"They only broke up 'cos he requested a work transfer to Vermont to get away from her," Maude filled in with a laugh, which Heather took as meaning that she'd just finished the newest level of her phone game.

Danni rolled her eyes. "No, he wasn't trying to get away from me. It was an actual work transfer."

Heather said, "So, yeah, why is it that if we're visiting your boyfriend—"

"Ex-boyfriend."

Heather shrugged. "Whatever. I can read that expectant look on your face like you're a book—you're on your way to get laid for sure. What I wanna know is, how is it that if we're on our way to visit your guy—"

"Ex-guy. You gotta get that small detail right. And I might not get laid. I think he's got a new girlfriend now."

"You *think?*"

Maude answered for her: "Well on Facebook, Ray keeps posting pictures of himself and this skanky redhead, but his profile doesn't say he's in a relationship with anyone."

"Alright," Heather agreed. "So you may or may not be getting some dick over the next two days, but that still doesn't answer my question—"

"Which you haven't even asked yet," Katie pointed out with a pained look on her face. Her gaze was fixed on the highway, but she seemed to be in some discomfort.

"Because she keeps interrupting me with corrections about the state of the relationship."

"What's the question anyway?" Maude asked.

"I'm curious as to why Danni is sitting in the backseat endlessly updating her Instagram status while I'm sitting here in the front seat, trying to work out where we're going."

"Oh that," Danni replied with a yawn that revealed the metal braces on her teeth. "Katie knows her way around these parts. Her folks used to live up—"

All of a sudden the pickup truck rolled to the side of the road and came to a halt.

Danni watched Katie put the gearshift in Park, then she leaned forward between the seats to stare at her. "Hey, what's happened?"

"We haven't just broken down, have we?" Maude added, looking out of the truck window with a shiver.

"What's the matter? You frightened of a few trees?" Danni teased.

"Only in your nightmares, honey."

Heather too stared over at their driver. "What's the matter? Have we run out of gas?"

Katie shook her head. "Nah, nothing that drastic. I just gotta take a shit, that's all."

"Can't it wait?" Maude asked. "It's creepy out here, just us in the woods and no cars passing."

"Not unless you don't mind me crapping my pants while driving." Katie was already opening the driver's side door. She leapt down and shut the door, then leaned back in to address the other young women. She was gripping her belly and grimacing like she was really hurting. "I think it was that fish sandwich I had for lunch. The fish tasted off, but I didn't wanna waste it."

Katie hurried around the front of the vehicle and started walking off into the trees.

"Hey, what about some toilet paper?" Heather called after her. "I've some in my purse."

"I'll use leaves," Katie called back as she vanished into the greenery.

"Watch out for monsters!" Maude shouted. "If something eats you in there there'll be a delay in Danni's getting laid!"

But Katie was already gone.

"I guess the girl just had to go," Danni said and returned her attention to her phone, opening Facebook and starting to scroll down her new notifications. Maude resumed playing her online game, her brow quickly furrowing up in concentration.

Heather was left alone with her thoughts. She didn't share Maude's worries. Sure they were somewhere in the middle of northwest MA, but they weren't lost—Katie's GPS had been giving them steady directions. At least it had been until a few miles from Deerfield, when Katie had decided that taking a shortcut instead of following the I-91 interstate like they'd been doing would shave a whole hour off their journey, and had then switched the device off. But neglected or not, the GPS on the dashboard still worked and would tell them their current location at the flick of a switch. And they all had signals on their cellphones; she pulled out hers for a look.

Yeah, I can call anyone I want and Danni's on Facebook, so we're not cut off from civilization. We've nothing to worry about.

But clearly, the fact that Heather was having to reassure herself that things were fine meant she was worried that they weren't. But maybe it was just that she was used to hearing creepy tales of people vanishing in the woods.

All I'm really worried about now is that the smell of Katie's poop might attract something dangerous—like a bear or a wolf—to come attack her.

Staring out of the green pickup truck at the trees on both sides of the road and the black line of tarmac that split them like an infected wound, she tried to remember if there were bears and wolves in this part of Massachusetts. She couldn't remember. She considered googling for an answer, but then she realized that if the answer was affirmative, she'd start worrying about Katie's safety.

She's just gone to take a crap, dammit! Nothing's gonna happen to her! What the hell am I so worried about?

Behind her, Danni and Maude were both clearly oblivious to her concerns. Danni was sighing about something.

"Dammit," Danni said, elbowing Maude, who now removed her earphones.

"What? Shit, you've made me drop that white block. What's up? Is Katie back?"

"Nah, Jack and Ashley just broke up."

"That's news? I told you it would never work—he drinks too much." She growled at Danni and replaced her earphones. "And please, don't poke me again. You shot up my concentration. Now I have to restart the level."

"Oh, sorry."

Silence returned to the backseat.

Heather considered browsing through Facebook herself, then decided against it. Instead, she shut her eyes and relaxed back in her seat, letting the cool evening breeze calm her.

Yes, this trip was just what she needed to relax after a hectic week at work.

CHAPTER 2

Ensemble, a.k.a the Compressed Character Meet & Greet

Katie Hemingway, Heather Forrest, Maude Mason and Danni Melcher were all from Raynham, Massachusetts. In fact they all lived in the same building on Britton Street. It was a large old house and was situated just a short distance from the Raynham Walmart Supercenter on lower Broadway, where Heather, Katie and Danni worked. Maude was the receptionist at the Dragon Nails Spa located along Raynham's New State Highway.

All four girls were in their early twenties. Katie and Heather were both twenty-one; Maude and Danni, twenty-two.

Physically the four young women looked alike. All four were attractive in their own ways, with Maude being the tallest and Danni the shortest; and Heather and Katie somewhere in-between them both.

Heather was bordering on plump; Katie had stretch marks from a teenage pregnancy that had resulted in a stillborn child; Danni wore braces; Maude had a big nose and enjoyed playing online games—everything from *Tetris* to *Home Street*.

Katie, Heather and Danni were brunettes, Maude was a redhead. Katie had blue eyes; Heather and Danni's eyes were brown, and Maude's were leaf-green.

None of the four of them liked rock music. Katie like C&W, Maude and Danni were into old-school techno and Heather liked smooth R&B. Heather adored R. Kelly, which meant she was very pissed off by all R. Kelly's current legal troubles as it meant she felt unpleasantly conspicuous now when playing her favorite songs of his.

Heather was even-tempered; Danni was super-smart and a bit of a nerd; Maude was an emotional time bomb, an explosion waiting to happen; and Katie was simply hard to place, a little bit of everything at the wrong or right place and time.

None of the four of them currently had a boyfriend. Heather simply didn't have one at the moment and was looking for someone who'd really love her. Danni was overly picky where men were concerned (brimming over with intelligence and self-confidence herself, she was into brains and not brawn). Katie claimed not to have the time for romance. And Maude? Well, Maude had no shortage of male admirers, with her hot figure and smoky green eyes, but she was such a combative young beauty that she ran them all off almost as fast as she attracted them.

So these, in a nutshell, were the four young female friends who set out on that fateful summer day's trip up north to the Green Mountain State.

The idea to make the trip was Danni's. And Danni's real reason for suggesting they travel to visit Ray Jackson up in Vermont was because she'd been unable to find a satisfactory replacement lover after she and he had split up—the problem wasn't the sex, but the presex/aftersex conversation. And now that she'd begun seeing photos of Ray and that airhead redhead ("Is it just me, or does your ex-bae have a thing for fire-crotches?" Danni had cattily asked.), she'd felt she'd better get on the scene quickly and break them up.

Katie had a ride. Katie agreed to drive Danni up to Vermont if she'd pay for gas. Danni readily agreed. Danni, wanting to have the advantage of numbers on her side when on her romantic opponent's home turf, also suggested that Heather and Maude come along. Heather had nothing doing over the weekend and agreed. Danni then persuaded Maude to postpone her trio of dates with potential boyfriends to the next weekend.

And then, after each having arranged to work the morning shift that Friday, that late afternoon they all set off in Katie's old army-green pickup truck, which she said had been a present from her father.

CHAPTER 3

Heather

"Hey, girls, where the hell has Katie gotten to?"

Danni's voice jerked Heather back to alertness. Heather realized that she must have dozed off. She shook herself fully awake and leaned forward in her seat, rubbing her eyes as she did so.

"Huh?" she asked. "What?"

A quick glance back revealed that Maude was still playing her game. Danni, however, was once more leaning forward between the seats with a bothered look in her eyes. She waited until Heather was paying attention to her before explaining: "Katie isn't yet back. And she's been gone for over twenty minutes now."

"Shit," Heather said.

"Maybe she's got a serious case of the runs," Maude suggested. Having lost the game level she was playing, she had decided to give up her digital warfare for a while and rethink her battle strategy.

"No," Danni said. "I don't think that's it."

"Aw heck," Maude said. "Something hasn't happened to her, has it?"

Heather sighed and pushed open the pickup truck's front passenger side door. "That's what we're gonna go find out."

They disembarked and then stood by the truck for a while. Three young women in tee shirts and denim pants (Maude had on denim shorts) and flip-flops, trying to make up their minds on their next course of action.

"Stopping here to take a crap was a crappy stop," Danni said. "We should have prevented Katie from going into the woods."

"She threatened to shit up the truck," Maude reminded her.

"It's her damn truck—we should have let her; poop smell isn't poison gas. We just wouldn't help clean it later."

Heather placed her hands on the shoulders of the other two girls. "Stop it. There's clearly a problem. We have to go into the woods and look for her."

Maude looked nervously at the twin walls of greenery that flanked the three of them, then pointed down the highway, then looked back the other way. At this point where they'd stopped, the road was a straight line and was empty in both directions. "Maybe we should wait for someone to come along, so we'll have some backup."

"Or just yell for Katie to move her ass," Danni suggested. Then she giggled. "Okay, I didn't quite mean that like that. She's already moving her ass in there."

Heather gaped at them both. "What on earth are both of you so frightened of? Being attacked by her poop?"

"Maybe we should just call the police?" Maude suggested.

Heather shook her head emphatically to that suggestion. "And have them get here to discover that Katie merely had the runs? No, thank you."

"Count me out of that one too," Danni seconded Heather.

"Guys, I don't feel good about this. I feel very uneasy here. I really think we'd be better off just calling the police to come handle this."

Danni smirked and pointed to Maude's cellphone. "All the *Spygirl* you keep playing is making you paranoid."

Heather shook her head. "No. She plays *Spygirl* because she's already paranoid. Killing an imaginary enemy helps balance her psyche." Then she scowled. "Guys, we can't just wait here." She swiped on her cellphone screen. "It's seven-thirty now. Night's coming on. Let's just enter the woods and find Katie and get ourselves back into her truck and get the hell away from here."

Maude shook her head. Now, rather than being frightened, she looked to be getting angry. "Hey, you two go. I'm waiting right here."

Danni strode to the edge of the forest calling, "Katie! Katie! Are you alright in there or has your poop eaten you!? Hey, Katie, can you hear me!?" While shouting, she squinted into the dimness beneath the trees, searching for a glimpse of either Katie's pink top or her denim pants.

There was no response from the forest other than a slight rustling of the leaves of the closest trees as summer breezes blew through their branches.

"Hey, Katie, what's going on in there!? Are you alright!?" Danni shouted some more and then turned to stare at the others. "Well, I guess that means no, she isn't alright."

"Or she's too far away in the woods to hear us calling her," Maude said.

"This isn't getting us anywhere," Heather said, pacing back and forth by the truck's hood, while Maude sat perched on the vehicle's front bumper and Danni leaned herself against its front passenger side door. "Katie's clearly in some danger, and the longer we stand here waiting, the greater the chance there is of her being abducted or worse still, being dead by the time we get to her." She looked angrily at her two companions. "Alright, both of you hens wait here, *I'll* go look for her."

"I'll go with you . . ." Danni began saying but was then interrupted by Maude, who said: "Hey, guys, someone's coming. Maybe he can help us."

Heather stopped her pacing. She and Danni both turned to look at the man whom Maude had noticed. The man was walking out of the woods on the other side of the road. He looked like a farmer. He was about six feet tall and very muscular, and was wearing dirty overalls and muddy boots. His hair was brown and he had a short beard. He didn't seem to have noticed the three of them yet.

Maude figured the man had come from a nearby farm. "Hey, mister, can you help us?" she called out as he stepped into the road.

This did get his attention. The man turned and stared at the three of them. They had sufficient time to notice that his eyes were very dark and were set extremely deep in their sockets, and then the strangest thing happened:

Quicker than the three young women could blink, the man changed shape. His body seemed to contract, with his faded blue clothes and boots transforming into gray-brown skin as it did so. His now bare arms and legs became shorter and thinner till they were almost as skinny as twigs and were tipped with long black claws. His head compacted to a diamond snakehead shape on a long neck, with the difference that it had only a single red eye, an eye with a pinprick black pupil, and one that seemed swollen with blood and ready to burst from its own internal pressure.

"What the fuck?" On witnessing this horrifying transformation, Heather had a sense of time slowing down, like during a car crash. It was strange . . . but, at the moment, she felt intense relief that this was real life.

"Oh shit," Maude said, crossing herself vigorously. "I just knew we should never have stopped here."

"Ssssh!" Danni said. "It's watching us!"

The creature in the middle of the road stared at the three of them for a moment, then it bared its teeth at them. It had lots of teeth, like shiny upright nails in its mouth, and a long pink tongue too. Its tongue dangled out of its mouth and dripped thick saliva on the road. Both its bony chest and its nostrils swelled and contracted with its loud breathing. It seemed crouched in an attack pose on those hind legs that, while not quite a beast's, were definitely no longer human. Even more horrifying, its wrinkled brownish body had dark red splotches on it that looked like bloodstains.

"What are we gonna do if this thing attacks us?" Heather whispered. "We haven't any weapons."

"Everyone start retreating towards the truck's doors," Danni whispered back. "Slowly, so we don't alarm it."

And so, trembling with fear, the three of them started backing away from the monster.

But then the monster in the highway abruptly turned away from them and ran off into the trees. They watched it go with relief.

"Fuck," Danni said. "What the hell just happened? What was that thing?"

"I feel like I'm frigging dreaming," Maude said. "Thank God it's gone. Now we three need to find Katie and be gone too before it comes back again."

"Yeah, did you see all those teeth? I almost peed myself."

"I felt like I'd just walked into a really bad dream."

"Guys, now we've a new problem," Heather said when she'd stopped trembling. She waited till she had both Danni and Maude's full attention, then spelt things out very simply for them so that there would be no silly arguments over the course of action she'd realized they now had to take: "And the problem is, when the monster ran off, it didn't go back the way it came. No, it entered *our* side of the woods . . . the same side as Katie went to poop." She let her words sink in, before adding, "And so, we can't wait anymore. We need to go in after it and get Katie out of there . . . before . . ."

That more or less settled it. There were no protests.

"We need weapons," Maude said.

"There's a tire iron in the back of the truck and some wrenches," Heather said. "And we'll keep our eyes open for any broken branches under the trees that might come in handy."

Once armed, they stepped under the trees and went looking for Katie. Heather, who was in the lead, had the tire iron and she soon picked up a baseball-bat-sized branch from the forest floor also. Danni carried two wrenches, her fingers tight about their grips. Maude was carrying a two-by-four they'd also found in the back of Katie's truck. This piece of wood had originally been in Danni's possession, but she'd quickly realized that she'd be unable to wield it properly in a conflict and so had handed it over to Maude who, being taller, had larger hands.

"What the hell do you think that horrible thing was?" Maude asked nervously. "Was that a werewolf?"

"Didn't look like a werewolf to me," Danni said. "It just looked fucked-up—like some mutant thing. Half teenager and half whatever."

Maude pushed branches out of her way, then winced when a twig snapped loudly beneath her flip-flops. "What sort of monster only has one eye?"

"A Cyclops?"

"That's Greek melodrama, nerd. I mean something *American*."

"Beats me."

"Shush, both of you," Heather cautioned with a finger across her lips. "We don't want the damn thing to hear us coming."

"Actually we do," Maude said. "So that it'll be gone by the time we get to wherever it was."

Heather stared grimly at Maude. Danni shrugged. "Em . . . she does have a point. With all those teeth it had, we're actually better off scaring it away than having to fight it."

"Whichever." They were moving deeper under the tree cover now, with the pickup truck hardly visible when they looked back because of the dense foliage in the way; or maybe they were even seeing its army-green shell but mistaking it for part of the forest. Up ahead was yet more leafy greenery and no sign of their missing friend.

Once her two companions were silent again, Heather began calling softly, "Hey, Katie, where are you? Katie, are you okay?"

"Now this is super-weird," Danni said when Heather's calls brought no response. "Yes, I know we can't *see* her, but shouldn't we be able to *smell* the stink of her poop by now?"

Heather turned and stared at Danni. The expression on her face said it all: Yes, this had become super-weird. "Alright, now I'm really becoming worried. We search for five minutes more and then call the police, alright?"

"Yeah," Danni and Maude quickly agreed.

Slowing their pace almost to a crawl now, they resumed searching.

CHAPTER 4

Hank

About twenty miles away from where the three young women from Raynham were searching for the fourth member of their traveling party, a man sat smoking in the front of a Jeep Cherokee. The man was middle-aged and had thinning hair that was the same ink-black as his Jeep, but unlike his new vehicle he had clearly seen a lot of personal wear and tear. In fact, the man seemed run down and neglected. And to a large degree this was the actual situation of things.

The man's name was Hank Rollins. He lived in the nearby town of Hinsdale and worked in a bank in the city of Pittsfield. But at the moment Hank Rollins was on a two-week summer vacation, which he'd figured would be time enough to do what he had to do.

Hank's Jeep was parked well off the road, in a clearing in the middle of the thick forest at the foot of Misery Mountain, which bordered New York State. This was the exact same spot that the vehicle had been parked the last time Hank had visited here. That had been two months ago, when he'd driven out here to picnic with his wife Josephine and to do some fly fishing with their teenaged son Hank Jr.

Hank Rollins Snr. wasn't married anymore, nor was he a father anymore. That last trip to this place had changed his life for the worst.

Misery Mountain had turned out to be more to be a mere appellation, it had become a deep symbol of the current miserable state of Hank's life.

In the two months since that last visit here, Hank had barely been holding onto his sanity, getting through each day only because he figured there was no point in committing suicide until he'd gotten revenge on the thing that had robbed him of his family.

Hank was here now to hunt it down.

He finished his cigarette and peered into the back of the Jeep, nodding down at the bundle in the rear footwell. After deciding that everything was in good condition back there, he lit himself another cigarette, opened up a can of beer, and frowned to himself.

Yes, I'm going to get that sonofabitch this weekend. Yes, I most certainly will.

***

Two months. A mere sixty days. Hank Rollins found it crazy how much one's life could alter in such a short period of time.

Married for nineteen years, he and Josephine had been happy together. He had a good job at the bank and for the first time in years, their finances had been in great shape. Hank Jr. had just graduated high school and his parents had had great hopes of him someday becoming a neurosurgeon.

And then had come that ill-fated fishing trip into the woods. Usually father and son went fishing alone, while Josephine spent the time visiting her friends. But this time, mainly because Josephine was worried that Hank Jr. had been growing away from her for years and that once pre-med school started he'd be gone for good and so she needed to fill this interim with memories of the happy times when she still had her son completely to herself, Josephine had insisted on coming along too.

The weekend trip had gone smoother than Hank expected. That Saturday they'd pitched their tent in the woods at the foot of Misery Mountain, by the bank of one of the many small rivers that watered the western part of the state. His worries that Josephine would soon start bitching about the mosquitos and her boredom never materialized. While he and the kid fished, she lay on a deck chair on the grassy riverbank and read a novel. (Hank could recall the book's title even now: The Sex Change Police by Arthur Wright Author.) Occasionally, she got up to fetch them all drinks. That Saturday evening they'd caught a lot of fish but threw most of them back into the river. Josephine cooked the rest for dinner.

That night the weather had been warm and they'd all slept out in the open, staring up at the moon while the river gurgled peacefully along a few feet away from them.

Hank had woken up the next morning to the sound of his son on the phone to his girlfriend and the pleasant sight of his wife emerging half nude from a swim in the river. They'd breakfasted on the remains of last night's dinner and then everyone got back to doing what they were here for, meaning Josephine resumed reading and her menfolk resumed fishing.

"You know," Josephine said with some regret after a while, "I should have come fishing more often with you two."

"It's never too late to start," Hank had said with a laugh. "Once Junior is off to med school we can both move out here for good."

It was on this Sunday morning that everything went bad.

At about 10 a.m. Hank had left the riverbank and walked back through the woods to get the fish cooler from the Jeep. He'd not bothered to carry it over yesterday because they'd planned to eat yesterday's catch. But now he needed the cooler to prevent today's catch from spoiling before they could get it home to the freezer.

He'd just gotten the cooler out of the Jeep's trunk when he heard a scream. Startled by the noise, he'd put down the cooler and listened carefully. The scream seemed to have come from where he'd left his family. He waited. Almost immediately there was another loud scream, then a third. He couldn't be certain that was Josephine's voice, but it sure as hell sounded like it.

Cursing himself for leaving his family alone, and also for parking a quarter of a mile away from the river, Hank set off running for the river again. He left the cooler behind.

His one thought while running was to get to the tent and get his shotgun. He crashed through the forest undergrowth, not caring when low-hanging branches whipped and tore his face with their leaves. Ahead of him the screaming intensified. Now he could tell that it *was* Josephine screaming, her terrified voice finally becoming a single sustained "NOOOOOOOO!" that at first rose like a rocket man and then plummeted like a lead zeppelin.

Hank finally crashed out beside the riverbank and couldn't believe what he was looking at.

His teenaged son lay on his back with his head in the river, his head completely under the shallow water by the riverbank. He was still alive, but only just. The kid was a bloody mess, with his belly torn open and his intestines spread to the left and right of him.

Junior's chest heaved with its desperate effort of trying to keep him alive while preventing him from breathing in water; he kept blowing bubbles up to the river's surface. The boy was twitching, his fingers feebly clawing the riverbank mud and trying to pull him out of the water but lacking sufficient strength to accomplish this desperate task.

Junior was lying directly in Hank's line of vision as he emerged from the trees, and so Hank saw this first of all. In ordinary circumstances, he would have instantly rushed to pull his son out of the water, but right now there was worse happening even closer to him.

His wife Josephine lay spread-eagled on her back on the forest grass, with her belly also ripped apart; and something was eating her guts. Josephine was dead—her face wrapped up in her long blond hair.

The thing eating Josephine's intestines was smallish but muscular with rough grayish-brown skin and with very thin limbs that ended in long black claws. Its head was snakelike. When it raised its bloody head to stare at Hank, he saw that it had just a single red eye like a huge tomato in the center of its forehead and that its huge mouth was full of needlelike but thick teeth.

The monster made a move towards Hank, but Hank had already gotten over the paralysis forced on him by his first sight of the creature. Before it could reach him, he'd leapt inside the tent and grabbed up the pump-action shotgun. Thinking he sensed the monster behind him, he'd spun around and let off a shotgun blast that ripped out half of the tent's left wall.

However, the tent was empty. He did hear a loud shriek from outside the tent—either of fear or pain—but when he ran out to see, the monster had vanished. But the damn thing had taken souvenirs: both Josephine's and Junior's bellies were completely empty of intestines; both had been totally excavated.

Completely horrified now, Hank had dropped the shotgun and pulled out his cellphone.

"Hello, this is 911, what is your emergency?"

"My family! My wife . . . my son! Something . . . something has killed them!"

"Where are you, sir?"

"In the woods near Misery Mountain . . . near a river . . . by one of the turnoffs off State Route 43. . . . I can't be more specific than that! Track my phone! My black Jeep is parked near the road! Please hurry!"

That information given, Hank's heart had given out on him and he'd suffered a good old-fashioned heart attack.

***

Hank's heart attack hadn't killed him—the paramedics arrived before it did and got him to the ER on time.

In fact, Hank's heart attack ironically saved him from doing jail time.

Because there was a problem.

See, when the police arrived at the scene after tracking Hank's cellphone signal, they didn't find any bodies. They found a lot of gore—bits of intestines and viscera and blood—splashed all over the grass, but no bodies. They found Hank lying on his belly by the tent entrance with a rock-cut in his cheek that assured them that he'd fallen straight forward on his face. But no dead wife or son. But DNA analysis proved that the spilled blood did indeed belong to Josephine Rollins and Harry Rollins Jr., and there was so much of it spilled that neither of the missing pair could still be alive. There was also the deep indentation of a body shape in the blood spilled by the riverbank, which confirmed that even if the dead teenager hadn't bled to death he'd have drowned to death anyway.

But where were the corpses?

When they got Hank stabilized in the ICU, he had no idea either.

When he described the thing he'd seen feeding on Josephine, the doctors and detectives thought he was delirious. When he insisted that he wasn't, the doctors explained that they meant he'd *been* delirious back then. He had after all suffered a heart attack, and it was very likely that, triggered by the unfamiliar exertion he'd put on his ticker during his wild dash through the woods from his Jeep to the riverbank, his heart attack had already been in progress by the time he'd burst out into the riverside clearing, meaning oxygen-deprivation to his brain had had him seeing things.

Hank didn't believe that at all, but no one believed him either, so he'd kept his thoughts to himself.

There was, of course, the suspicion that *he'd* murdered his family.

But this was quickly disproved. The primary evidence in his favor was that there was none of the two victims' blood anywhere on him. And as the cops had quickly pointed out to themselves, there was absolutely no way that Hank could have killed two people as bloodily as his missing wife and son must have been murdered without getting blood-soaked himself.

***

Hank was discharged after a week in hospital.

As he'd expected, once he'd been ruled out as a suspect, investigations into Josephine and Junior's disappearances/murders just stalled. The police had no evidence and so the case was still open.

Hank, however, intended to close the case this weekend.

He was here in these woods now to hunt the damn monster down.

Hank had a plan to catch the monster. And he didn't see his plan failing.

CHAPTER 5

The Girls

Their ears peeled for sounds of both Katie and the monster, Heather, Danni and Maude inched their way through the forest.

After a while, Heather called a halt. "Guys, wait. We've seen no signs that Katie came this way."

"Yeah," Danni nervously agreed. "Now I'm certain something's happened to her."

"I suggest we stop searching right now and call the cops," Maude said, leaning against a tree after first looking suspiciously up into its branches to ensure they contained nothing that could fall on her.

"Yeah, I guess you guys are right." Heather got her phone out.

"Hey wait!" Maude said as Heather was about dialing.

"Yes?"

"Remember not to mention that crazy monster we saw, or they'll think we're just pranking them and won't turn up."

Heather nodded and tapped the '9' on her keypad.

"Wait! Don't!" This time it was Danni who'd protested.

Heather looked at her, her gaze a little irritated now. "What is it?"

Danni looked embarrassed while she explained: "Well, don't you think we should try calling Katie's phone first before getting the cops involved?"

Heather looked surprised at the suggestion. "I thought she left it in the truck."

"I'm sure she didn't," Danni said. "Look, give me a moment to call her first, then you can call the police afterwards."

But before Danni could make the call, her cellphone rang anyway.

"Is it Katie?" Maude asked expectantly.

"No, it's Ray. Shush!"

A smile breaking out on her face, Danni put the cellphone to her ear. "Oh hi, Ray. . . . Huh? . . . Yeah, we're on our way over. . . . Where? . . . Hold on a moment while I ask Heather."

She lowered the phone and looked at Heather. "Where exactly are we now?"

Heather shrugged. "No idea."

Danni's glance at Maude produced another perplexed shrug. Shrugging back at them, she put the phone back to her ear again. "Sorry, no one knows for sure. I just know we're somewhere in northwest Massachusetts, along some shortcut that Katie suggested so we'd get to your place early. Katie? . . . Oh, she got out to take a dump and now we can't find her and . . . Yeah sure, we'll be careful and watch out for bears. Oh, man, you wouldn't believe what just happened to us . . ." Then she caught the frown on Heather's face, along with the neck-slicing gesture that Maude was making with her left hand. "Sorry, gotta hang up now. We need to resume looking for Katie. Tell you what happened when we reach Searsburg."

"The way you were talking, I thought you planned on having phone sex with him," Maude said after Danni hung up.

Danni made a face at her. "Okay, time to try Katie's number."

This time it was Heather's phone that rang before Danni could dial. "It's Katie," she told them with relief, then accepted the call.

"Katie, where are you? . . . In the woods near the truck, looking for us? . . . Where are *we?* We're looking for you. . . . No, we can't see the road from here, too many damn trees in the way. . . . You can't see us either? . . . Yeah, we're coming."

Heather hung up and then looked at her two friends. "I don't know what happened, but she's behind us now."

"I don't think it matters what happened," Maude said. "Just so long as we get out of here already.

"See?" Danni said with relief. "Just imagine what would've happened had you called the cops and all they needed to do to find Katie was make a phone call."

Maude was already walking off towards the highway. The others followed. About fifty yards later, they saw Katie standing beside a tree trunk and waving at them. They were all surprised to see the revolver she was holding. Katie seemed amused at their makeshift armory of tire iron, wrenches and plank.

They hurried over to her side. "Where'd you get that gun?" Danni asked.

"I always keep it under the front seat in case of emergencies."

"How come you never mentioned it before?" Maude asked suspiciously.

" 'Cos I didn't want you removing it without my knowledge to go shoot some ex-lover you're pissed off with? I wasn't gonna take it out at all, 'cept that I saw something crazy dash through the woods while I was relieving myself a little while ago."

"Hey—you saw it too?"

"Looked like a skinny monkey with a snake's head. I must've been hallucinating though. But still, I got the gun out for safety's sake."

"No, it was real."

"Ah, whatever." Katie spun away from them and then waved a hand back at them, gesturing that they follow her. "C'mon, let's get the hell out of here." Her voice had a sudden cold edge to it as if she was annoyed with her mind for playing tricks on her.

Katie led the way through the trees and the other young woman followed her. The sky, as much of it as they could see through the tree cover, had turned grayish now. Nightfall wasn't that far off.

"Dammit, I'm glad that's over," Heather said when they'd once more emerged by the highway.

"Yeah," Danni agreed. "I kept expecting that weird creature to drop down on me from one of the trees."

"Me too," Maude said, skipping ahead of the others to the pickup truck and waiting for them to catch up. Leaning with both hands on her two-by-four beside the front passenger window, she turned back towards her friends and added, "And, Katie, for heaven's sake, next time pick a shortcut that people actually use."

And then she frowned at them. "What are you guys looking so surprised about?"

But they weren't looking at her, but rather past her. So, fearing that the shapeshifting monster had returned and was now right behind her, Maude spun around and saw what her three friends were staring at.

Two men were standing on the other side of their vehicle. Both had apparently been squatting on its blindside, hiding from the girls as they emerged from the woods. Alarmingly, both of the men were armed with shotguns. Even more alarming than this was how the men looked. One of them was extremely tall, a giant, while the other was a dwarf, his head barely reaching the chest of his companion. Both men were extremely well-muscled however, had short black hair and were clean-shaven.

"Hello, ladies," the short man said, stepping around the front of the truck, with the giant one following behind him. They both wore dirty denim overalls, though the giant's clothes were several sizes too small for him.

"Who-who-who are y-y-you?" Maude stuttered, leaping away from the pickup truck.

"Yes and what do you want with us?" Heather asked, more confidently than Maude. "We're just traveling through to Vermont."

"Well, I can assure you fine girls that your weekend joyride just ended," the short man said. Up close, he had a very evil face, one that was lined and dirty and jaded. Age-wise, he looked to be in his early thirties. His nose was very small and his eyes quite large. His lips were extremely thin and barely covered his teeth, which were as brown as if he'd never heard of toothpaste in his life.

The taller (and younger) man's eyes didn't match each other and also had something moronic in their gaze—he stared a lot as if he was mentally retarded. His lips were quite thick and when he opened his mouth and yawned, they saw that his teeth were dirty too. Both men had dirty, grubby hands with cracked fingernails, and clear sky-blue eyes.

"Alright, now, first of all," the dwarf went on, "you girls all drop those weapons you're holding."

"Huh?" Because Katie was the only one of them with a gun, it took the other three young women a while to understand what he was referring to, but then Heather dropped the tire iron, Danni dropped her two wrenches, and Maude reluctantly let go of her hefty two-by-four. The sound of the 'weapons' hitting the grassy highway verge filled Heather with really bad anticipation. They'd just let go of the only protection that they had.

Because Heather was standing slightly in front of Katie, she couldn't see if Katie had dropped her gun too or if she'd been able to conceal it before the men noticed it. She clung to a slight hope that the latter was the case.

"Hey, we're not looking for any trouble," Maude said, her voice transforming from worried/scared to angry. This was the thing with Maude. Once worked up, she was like a Porsche sports car with great acceleration—zero to sixty mph in three seconds flat. Also, even though these were really scary men, they were still just *men*, and Maude was used to dealing with men. She'd put lots of jerks in their place.

The dwarf laughed and shifted his shotgun to cover Maude. He was really short, barely five feet in height. All four girls were taller than him, including Danni who was the shortest of them.

He said, "Well, well, ladies, you might not be looking for trouble, but you sure as hell have found it now." He laughed louder and then asked, "Ain't that right, sis?"

"Yeah, it sure is," Katie replied.

Sis? The three girls turned and gaped at Katie, who'd stepped behind them during their confusion. Now they discovered that she was pointing her revolver at them and was grinning coldly.

"These two are your brothers?" Maude asked. "You're family?"

Katie sniggered. "Yes, though I daresay there ain't much of a family resemblance. But turn around, bitches, and let me introduce you." She waited until her three friends had done so, and then went on: "Alright, the tall one is my younger brother Six-Six—that's his exact height, six feet, six inches—while the dwarf—"

"Hey, quit that! I ain't no damn dwarf!"

". . . Is my older brother Runt—so named for obvious reasons."

"Yeah, that's right," Runt said in some irritation. "Like being short is the end of the damn universe. Just don't go calling me a damn dwarf again."

"And you three girls have just been kidnapped," Katie said.

"I can't believe you set us up," Danni said in disbelief.

"Believe it, bitch," Katie said. Her voice was frigid, but tinged with amusement.

"You're supposed to be our *friend*," Maude accused her. "You're one of my closest friends. I confide in you about everything."

Katie laughed now. "That's what I *wanted* you to think, you idiot. Who in their right senses wants to be best friends with a narcissistic slut like you? All you ever talk about is guys—you think 'dick' is a type of lipstick. Knowing you murders my brain cells."

Hurt filled Maude's eyes at these cutting words. She rounded on Katie. "You nasty bitch!"

Before either of the others could stop her, Maude leapt at Katie with her fingernails extended to scratch her eyes out.

Katie sidestepped Maude's lunge and then clubbed her on the head with her gun. The tall girl went down flat on her face. When she rolled over and sat up, she looked dazed and was bleeding from a cut on her left temple.

"You goddamn bitch," Maude wheezed. "I don't believe you just did that."

Katie knelt beside her and shoved the muzzle of her revolver all the way into Maude's open mouth, making her sputter and choke on the cold metal. "Start believing it, slut. You try one more stunt like that and I'll blow your brains out."

"Ha ha ha, yeah!" the giant Six-Six laughed, instantly confirming to the girls that he was mentally challenged. He laughed long and hard, with his face splitting in a wide grin and his shotgun swiveling from side to side as he did so. The gun looked like a toy in his massive hands.

Katie removed the gun barrel from Maude's mouth, and then, grabbing a fistful of Maude's red hair, she jerked her to her feet and shoved her forward into Danni. "Remember what I said: you piss me off just once more and I'll kill you right here and right now. And no one's gonna hear it happen, because no one ever drives up this way anymore."

Danni began silently crying, the tears streaming down her cheeks. Heather stepped up close to her and put an arm around her shoulders. "Don't worry," she whispered comfortingly. "Everything's going to be alright."

"No it ain't," Katie laughed right beside Heather's ear. "From this point onward, everything just gets much worse for you three bitches."

Heather had had no idea that Katie had heard her comforting Danni. She looked now at the thickset dwarf named Runt for confirmation of what Katie had said.

He laughed in her face. "Yeah, girl, that's just about right, what she just told you. All that you three pretty ladies have to look forward to now is a whole lot of pain and suffering."

Danni now began crying loudly. Maude stood half-stunned by the truck, looking as if she'd collapse at any moment.

"What do you want with us?" Heather asked. She'd been sizing up the situation, trying to work out their chances of escaping from Katie and the two men. At the moment that possibility looked really slim.

24

She didn't know exactly what their captors wanted from them, but it had to be really bad.

"What do you want with us?" she asked again.

Runt's lips creased up in an ugly smirk. "Well, first of all, you three girls had better all hand over your cellphones, and also any tablet devices you may be carryin' on yourselves."

Heather's heart sank at that request.

"Listen," Danni said tearfully, "just let us go. You can have all our phones and our money and stuff. Just don't hurt us."

The dwarf immediately shook his head and licked his lips. "No. Round up their phones, Katie."

Danni started crying again. Heather hugged her close. Maude just stared glumly at the green pickup truck's rear offside tire.

Katie stuck her revolver in her back pocket and quickly collected the other girls' cellphones. Maude put up a bit of a fight when Katie tried to take her phone from her pocket, but she let go of it when Katie slapped her.

Maude also had a laptop in her travelling bag. Katie got the laptop out and then carried it and the phones a short distance into the highway's grassy verge. Then she returned to their little gathering and winked at Runt. "Your shot, bro."

Leaving Katie covering their captives with her gun, Runt walked over to where the cellphones and laptop lay on the grass. Then, after first rearranging them into a rough pile with his boot, he stepped back and aimed his shotgun at them. Two shotgun blasts later—each of which made the three captive young women flinch and tremble with horror—and there was nothing left of the four devices.

"Well, I guess your trail ends here," Katie told her onetime supposed friends in amusement as her older brother walked back to join them. "You guys just became roadside disappearance statistics."

"Katie, what's gotten into you?" Heather asked. "I can't believe you're really doing this to us. You're supposed to be our friend."

"Damn well believe it, girl," Katie said, grabbing a fistful of Heather's brown hair and yanking her head forward with it, till Heather's face was close enough for her to kiss her if she wanted to.

"Ouch, let go of my hair! That hurts!"

Katie tugged even harder on her hair and smirked. "I already told you three dumb slits—I'm *not* your friend. I never was your friend. Everything we ever said and did together was all just playactin' on my part so that you three would trust me enough that you'd let me bring you up here. And that's——"

"Hey, it's gettin' late," Runt interrupted her, pulling her away from Heather with a firm hand on her shoulder. "Time we start gettin' a move on."

"Yeah, sis, we'd best be headin' home," the giant Six-Six agreed in a dopey drawl, this actually being the first thing he'd said other than all the laughing he'd done. Then he laughed some more and grinned lewdly at Heather, while grabbing his crotch, which was now sporting a large bulge, and squeezing hard. "Oh wow. She's so plump and juicy, must have a lovely pussy. I can't wait. I can't wait!"

"Control yourself, boy," Runt sternly told his huge brother. "Time enough for that soon."

The giant calmed down at little but kept licking his lips at Heather, which made her squirm with unease.

Runt meanwhile, was handing over what looked like sunglasses to their three captives.

"What are these for?" Danni asked, wiping the tears from her face.

"Put them on and you'll find out," Katie said menacingly, pausing in her task of picking up the tire iron and wrenches that the girls had discarded and returning them to the rear of her truck. "Hurry the fuck up."

Runt was less communicative than his sister. When Danni didn't don the sunglasses fast enough for his liking, he simply grabbed her by the throat with his muscular fingers and started choking her. Six-Six meanwhile laughed like an idiot and kept the captives covered with his shotgun. His crotch still bulged massively, like he'd stuffed a thanksgiving turkey in his underpants.

"Put the damn glasses on, bitch, before I crack you in the head with this two-by-four," Katie told Heather, who complied after giving her a look of pure hatred. A look which made only Katie laugh and add, "Oh yeah, wanna scrap, bitch? But there's nothing you can do, is there?"

Choking for breath, Danni had slipped the sunglasses on too and she instantly remarked. "Hey, I can't see a thing!"

Runt laughed and let go of her throat. "That's 'cos we painted the inside of the glasses with black paint."

"Why the hell would you do that?" Heather whimpered in fright.

"So ya don't see where we'se taking you cuties," Six-Six said in that moronic drawl of his. He leaned forward over Heather and ran the fingers of his left hand through her brown hair as if he was combing it for her. She flinched at his touch, but didn't dare shove him away.

"Yeah, the six of us are about going on a trip elsewhere," Katie explained. "And our destination's a top secret."

"Alright, now in you girls get." This said, Runt grabbed the sunglassed Maude and then opened the pickup's rear offside door and shoved her inside.

With Six-Six covering them with his shotgun to forestall any escape attempts, Katie herded Heather and Danni into the back of the vehicle also.

Runt then got in beside the captives and shut the door. He waited until Katie and Six-Six had gotten into the pickup truck's front seats and then said:

"Now, listen up, you three passengers. Those sunglasses mean you can't see where we're takin' you, but don't any of you start getting any ideas of escapin'." Danni was seated next to him and he jabbed her in the belly with a long hunting knife he pulled from his belt. He jabbed her lightly, but deep enough to slit her tee shirt and draw some blood. Danni yelped in pain.

"Stop hurting her!" Heather said.

In response to that, Runt jabbed the knife a bit deeper into Danni's belly. Still skin-deep though, not through into the muscle; just enough to make her bleed a little more.

This time Danni didn't cry out. She gasped, then moaned in terror and pain. Tears began dribbling down her face from behind her painted-out sunglasses.

Heather reached over and took Danni's hand. "Stop it! Stop it, please!" Maude, seated on Heather's other side, was silent, her body tensed up, her fingers curved into claws, as if she was thinking of leaning forward and ripping Katie's throat out. For the moment though, she did nothing, just simmered in place like a cooking pot doing its best not to boil over despite the burner being turned up to maximum.

Katie was now looking back between the seats with interest. "And no dipping your heads down and peeking over the top of the lenses," she said. " 'Cept you wanna bleed a lot. Remember, I can see you doin' that in my rearview."

As if emphasizing his sister's warning, Runt twisted the knife in Danni's side one more time. She gasped with pain, which caused Heather to turn her head towards her tormentor and plead: "Stop it, stop it, stop it! We'll do whatever you say."

"Yeah, we will," Maude hissed. "We promise we won't make any trouble."

"I think they mean it," Katie said.

Runt nodded. Katie turned back to face the steering wheel.

With a cold smile on his ugly face, Runt pulled the knife away from Danni, leaving her to slump back into the seat as if she'd fainted.

"Good," he said. "I think we understand ourselves now. You girls make one wrong move, or say one wrong thing if we get stopped by the State Police and I'll gut y'all like pigs."

"After we kill the law enforcement pigs first, of course," Six-Six said from the front seat, making all three siblings burst into demented laughter.

"So you girls just sit nice and pretty," Runt went on, "and you let us do all the talkin' if any cops stop us. If they ask you anything, you tell 'em we're all friends off on a weekend hunting trip in the mountains. You got that?"

Three nods from three temporarily blinded heads replied him. Three pairs of scared lips replied him: "Yes, yes."

Runt smirked coldly. "Alright, Katie let's go. It's about dinner time now and I'm downright starving."

"Me too," Six-Six said.

Katie started up the car and they drove off.

CHAPTER 6

Hank

After a last cigarette, Hank decided he was ready to start hunting the beast that had killed his wife and son.

He flicked the still glowing cigarette stub out of the Jeep's windows, then opened the door and got out. He stood there beside the door, gathering up his courage for what was to come. He stared down at the forest floor where the dropped cigarette glowed like a confused firefly. Feeling suddenly uneasy, Hank stomped it out.

Then he waited some more, keeping still as a rock and staring around at the surrounding trees, listening to ensure that he was still alone out here in the woods. He saw a few squirrels in the tree branches, but that was all. Slowly he relaxed.

It won't do for the monster I'm hunting to ambush me instead of the other way around, Hank thought grimly. *No, that won't do at all.*

Hank had a moment's unpleasant memory: the sight of Josephine dead, with that monster bent over her, its body red and wet with her blood and with coils of her intestines between its tearing and chewing teeth. As the image filled his mind, angry bile filled his throat and he felt the intense pain of his loss again.

I am going to kill that thing if it's the last thing I ever do!

Scowling in the twilight, he shut the driver's door and opened the rear one on that side. Then he tapped the burlap sack he'd spread out over the bundle down in the footwell.

"Hey, wake up, kid. It's time to get to work."

The sack didn't move, so Hank reached down and pulled it away, revealing the bound-up and gagged young man lying there. The boy was tightly trussed up in duct tape, with his hands bound behind his back and his knees and ankles also taped together. The young captive was 19-years-old. He had short blond hair and was dressed in a blue shirt and gray trousers, both of which were smeared with dirt and grease from him being hauled around by Hank. He was barefoot; his sneakers were back in Hank's living room.

The kid still seemed to be out cold. No, that wouldn't do. Hank needed the kid to walk to the campsite; out of shape like Hank was from sitting behind a bank desk all these years, there was no way in hell that he could either carry or drag him a half-mile through the woods.

Yes, I want to catch the damn monster, but I don't want to have a coronary while doing so. It's already given me one heart attack and I can do without another.

The kid was lying with his head next to Hank's legs, so Hank leaned over him and slapped him hard in the face. When that first slap produced no result, he slapped him again. The fifth slap more or less revived the kid. His eyes opened and then blinked while he remembered where he was.

"Time for work, son," Hank said. "We've a monster to catch."

The kid began squirming against his bonds, with loud groans coming from his taped-over mouth. He clearly wasn't at all in sympathy with Hank's plans. Particularly not the matter-of-fact way that Hank had just announced his intentions as if he was talking about catching trout.

"Now, don't be like that, son," Hank said, leaning in and gripping the young man under his shoulders and carefully easing him out of the back of the Jeep. "I already explained everything to you. Once we're through you can go home and I'll pay you for your help, alright? You'll even get a bonus. But not before."

These words clearly didn't reassure the kid, who instantly began thrashing about again.

"Hold still, you young punk!" Hank growled.

The kid, however, kept struggling to get free. But bound up in duct tape like he was, this proved to be very unwise. All he got for his efforts was to dislodge his captor's hands from under his shoulders, which resulted in Hank dropping him and he almost knocking himself out again when his head struck the forest floor. He lay there, half in, half out of the black vehicle, gasping for breath.

Hank shook his head at the kid. "Dumbass."

But the boy had unwittingly made the task of removing him from the Jeep easier. Hank had no further protests as he pulled the kid out of the Jeep and fully onto the forest floor. Then, while the young man weakly tried to escape the rolls of duct tape that Hank had bound him with, Hank got out the knapsack of food and supplies that he'd brought along for this hunting trip.

Last of all he got out his pump-action shotgun.

He waved the shotgun at the bound-up young man. It was just getting dark now and Hank liked the way that the fading daylight filtering through the tree cover glittered off the weapon's long barrel. Then he placed the shotgun on the ground beside him and pulled out a razor-sharp survival knife from the knapsack. He bent over the kid's legs and then changed his mind. Walking on his knees, he moved up towards the kid's face and placed the knife against his cheek.

"Now, listen, Jory. I'm going to untie both of your ankles now, and I'm also going to cut both of your knees free. But don't you dare get any stupid ideas about kicking me. If you do, you won't ever have sex again in your life, 'cos I'll cut your rod off. Alright?"

"Hmmmph! Hmmmph."

"Just nod if you understand me. *Do you* understand me?"

The kid nodded.

Hank nodded back. "Good. You don't do anything stupid tonight and we'll both leave here as safe and sound as when we arrived."

The kid nodded again. But from the way his eyes were gaping in fright, he clearly didn't believe a word that Hank was saying.

***

The kid's name was Jory Haines. Hank didn't know him from Adam. He'd just needed someone to use as monster bait. So yesterday night, he'd done what he figured anyone in his situation would do: he'd driven out to the nearby town of Worthington and parked behind the first open convenience store he came to. He'd then waited for some late-night stragglers to show up. His preferred choice would have been a woman, as he figured they'd be easier to scare and handle, but the few women who'd come to the store had been accompanied by their husbands or boyfriends.

Jory had come out last of all, right when Hank was already thinking he'd have to go the time-tested serial killer route and just hire a hooker for the night.

But then Jory had conveniently emerged from the rear of the convenience store.

It was only after knocking Jory out and stuffing him in the Jeep that Hank realized that Jory was actually the convenience store clerk and that there was going to be a search made for him when he didn't show up for work the next day. But by then it was too late to be helped. Hank had driven a short distance out of town, then parked and properly duct-taped the kid up before he woke up. Then he'd driven on home and locked the kid in the garage.

This morning he'd brought the boy into the house, explained to him why he'd abducted him, fed him at gunpoint and let him use the toilet. Then he'd settled down to wait for nightfall. He'd let the kid watch TV all day long, though he'd kept him well bound up with duct tape. Lots of superhero movies to relax him a little. He'd hooked them up to Netflix: *Avengers: Infinity War* and after that, *Thor: Ragnarok*, which seemed to make Jory forget he was a captive for a bit.

As a reply to the kid's question "Why are you doing this to me?" when he'd untaped his lips so he could eat breakfast, Hank had explained what had happened to his wife and son to Jory.

"Listen, I just need your help," he'd said. "And I'm gonna pay you well too," he'd assured the confused young man, waving a fat white envelope at him, then opening and fanning out its greenback content. "There's ten thousand dollars in here. Once our objective is achieved and I've caught my monster, I'll let you go and this cash is all yours. You can report me to the cops then. But I don't think you will, son. Not after being paid ten grand for a mere twenty-four-hour inconvenience. Or will you?"

Jory, once more gagged so he couldn't yell and alert the neighbors, had shaken his head. He was clearly interested in the money. Hank was certain that once he paid the boy off, he'd have no further complaints.

And so they'd sat out the day till evening, with Hank taking Jory to the bathroom every now and then for a pee, and also sticking a straw under the duct-tape covering his mouth so he could sip on a few beers to get himself in the mood.

And it seemed to be working too. By degrees, Jory seemed to have caught the spirit of the hunt; so much so that at one point the kid had laughed behind his gag at something on TV.

But then, just before they'd set out on this trip, Jory had become unruly again. Hank couldn't tell if this was because he'd given the kid too much beer to drink, or maybe too little beer to buck up his courage, or if the problem was that he'd given him too good a description of what they were up against.

So, regretfully then, because it made moving the kid a pain in the ass, Hank had had to knock Jory out again, and drag him out of the living room to the garage.

Which was why the kid had arrived in the woods unconscious.

***

Hank cut the tape around Jory's ankles and then that around his knees. Then he helped the boy up and shoved him towards the gap in the trees that led towards the river. "Alright, son, now you just walk ahead of me into those trees over there."

He watched the scared youth stumble reluctantly forward, then sensing he might make a run for it, called out: "Hey, not so fast. Wait right there, while I pick up my stuff and lock my car. You wouldn't want anything to rip out your guts if you got too far ahead of me now, would you?"

The kid waited. Hank made sure the Jeep Cherokee was locked up, then shouldered his backpack and picked up his shotgun.

He felt a twinge of conscience as he joined Jory by the makeshift path through the woods. The last of the daylight was fading now and as the forest clearing went from gray to black Hank saw that Jory was scared shitless. The kid was trembling. His face was grayer than a corpse's.

And he hasn't even seen the thing we're hunting yet.

Hmm. Maybe it wasn't right to bring this kid along. *Perhaps I should just have come alone. But this is a two-person job—one person to attract the beast, another to shoot it dead. Just like a fisherman, a hunter needs bait. And besides, I've got this covered. Other than for him maybe pooping his pants when the damn monster appears, no harm's gonna come to the kid.*

He frowned grimly and poked his shotgun in the middle of Jory's back. "Alright, son, get a move on. We've a monster to catch, and we haven't got all night to do it."

Jory seemed reluctant, so Hank jabbed him in the back again, more forcefully this time. "Hey, get your feet moving. We didn't come here to loiter about."

Jory began walking. Hank followed, flashlight in one hand, shotgun held ready in the other. The deeper they walked into the woods, the more tense Hank grew. He'd initially been full of confidence in his ability to catch this monster. But now he began worrying that he'd misjudged his own capabilities as a hunter. *What if something goes wrong? What if . . . what if . . . ?*

Hank felt relieved when they emerged beside the river, its waters dark and serene as the night came fully into its own.

CHAPTER 7

Heather

It was a long ride to their destination, long enough for the dying day to become dusk.

Because of the painted-over shades she was wearing, Heather was of course unable to see ahead of her. Her peripheral vision—the little she could make out outside of the glasses' rims—showed Maude's rigid body on her left and Danni's trembling chin and chest on her right. Occasionally she caught glimpses of the dwarf seated on Danni's right, his shotgun resting on his thighs and clasped in large and dirty fingers. Beyond her three backseat companions the trees existed for her as a green wall, with their monotony earlier broken up by the red or blue or white flash of a passing car going the other way. There'd been no such flashes for ten minutes now.

No police had stopped them either.

Their captors were silent. Katie had the radio playing some C&W station at low volume and she and Six-Six were humming along to the tunes.

Once Katie had asked: "Hey, guys, what was that crazy-looking thing that ran past me while I was hiding out in the woods like we'd agreed?"

Six-Six had replied with a laugh. "That? Oh, that's the *Gutter.*"

"The friggin' what?"

"We call it the 'Gutter' 'cos it eats guts—human guts," Runt said. "You'd better wait and ask Electra if you want a proper explanation."

That settled it. Katie had resumed humming along with the radio.

Heather had noticed the subtle (or maybe not so subtle) change in Katie's voice now that she was with her family. Her English had abruptly shifted (yes, not so subtle!) to much more informal lingo, at least while addressing her two dirty brothers.

And Electra? Electra? What kind of a name is that to have in the twenty-first century. Was their mother a fan of Greek mythology, or what? And in fact, who names their kids 'Six-Six' and 'Runt' anyway? In which case I'm certain that Katie's real name is something like 'Evil Bitch.'

Danni was sobbing quietly now, with just the occasional whimper escaping her mouth. Her body trembled as she gripped Heather's hand tight. The wound in her belly from Runt's knife seemed to have stopped bleeding. Heather patted Danni's hand, trying to reassure her as best she could. She didn't want to turn and whisper to her in case their captors took exception to her doing so. On her right, Heather could see Maude's brown fingernails tapping angrily on her knees.

How the hell did we wind up getting kidnapped by rednecks? And where the hell are they driving us to?

Yes, Heather was very scared but she was brave too. Even though she felt like curling up into a ball and hiding, she knew she needed to be strong now. Only thinking straight could help them now. Danni was too scared to do so, and Maude too angry. At first, when this ride had begun, Heather had expected Maude to open the rear door beside her and fling herself out into the highway, heedless of passing traffic. It was the sort of thing that Maude could do, and one which in these dire straits might actually have paid off. But Maude hadn't done so. Heather didn't know if this was because she'd not thought of it, or because Katie had the child-locks on.

I need to come up with some kind of a plan and quickly, Heather thought. *It would have been easier if I was sitting next to one of these rear doors. I could have tried opening it and spilling out into the highway. Sure, it may kill me, but . . . heck, it's even too late for that now.*

Heather figured that they'd been travelling for close to thirty minutes now. And for the past fifteen of those they'd been ascending, with Katie steering her army-green pickup truck first onto a highway turnoff and then off of that and onto one dirt road after another. The point was that they were obviously traveling further and further away from civilization. Heather determined the rural nature of these successive upward route transitions at first by the bumpy feel of the ground the vehicle was rolling over, and later by the additional smell of inclosing trees across their climbing route.

Katie's driving us up into the mountains! This made scary sense to her. Western Massachusetts was full of mountains.

Looking ahead into the painted sunshades was as good as closing her eyes, so Heather did close her eyes. A few seconds later, however, she jerked them open again in alarm. Leaning over Danni to reach her, Runt had just placed his hand on her right thigh and was fondling it.

Heather felt like screaming. Up till now she'd managed to ignore the muscular dwarf with the shotgun. With Danni seated between the two of them, this had proved easy enough, with her main reminder of the man's presence being his repulsive odor. Both he and his brother Six-Six smelt like they never took a bath. They also reeked of something like animal fat.

Danni had meanwhile frozen up like she wasn't even there with them in the truck's backseat. Heather could feel Danni's body trembling though, could feel her breathing hard and fast, as if she was terrified of being stabbed in the gut again.

Runt's thick fingers idly traced their way along Heather's thigh, stopping just short of her crotch, while he laughed like he was enjoying himself. Heather felt worms of revulsion crawling up and down her spine. She wanted to slap his hand away; to slap him too. All she did, however, was cross both hands tight over her crotch, so he couldn't touch her sex. She realized it was good that Maude wasn't the one sitting next to Danni. That would have been disastrous. If he'd touched Maude the way he was touching her now, Maude would have blown up. Her reaction might get her killed but she'd rip Runt's face open with her fingernails before he blew her head off.

Still laughing, Runt took his hand off of Heather's thigh and settled back in his place by the door. "Time enough to play later," he said. "But now, ladies, we're almost home."

This announcement brought a fresh spillage of tears from Danni. Heather reached over and squeezed her hand again.

She was aware that they'd stopped climbing the slope now. The pickup truck was rolling over level terrain, though the tree cover seemed thicker. Then they pulled out into a wide space—Heather's peripheral wall of trees suddenly pulled back from the vehicle—and the truck slowed to a halt.

Heather heard Katie click the gearshift into Park, and then Six-Six said, "Alright, girls, we'se home. You can take off your sunglasses now. Easy now, don't you break 'em—we need 'em for next time."

Heather was relieved to be able to see again. She slipped the horrid blacked-out sunglasses off her face, passed them forward to the giant and then stared out through both windshield and side windows to see where they were. Yes, they were in a wide clearing, and at quite an elevation too—even here in the truck the air smelt clean and very fresh and somehow thinner as well, though she instantly admitted that this last might be merely her imagination at work.

Heather couldn't tell for sure, because there were several trees in the way, but Katie seemed to have parked about twenty yards away from a house.

"Alright, everyone out," Runt said, breaking up her train of thought and then opening the door on his side and climbing down from the vehicle.

The three girls got out. Danni's eyes were red from weeping. Maude's face was reddish with anger.

Oops, she's had too much time to think about this. And the way she's looking at Katie . . .

No, the fight hadn't left Maude's eyes. She looked as if, given the chance, she'd tear Katie to shreds. Heather shuddered and resolved to try to keep Maude calm. She knew her friend very well. It would take just the slightest provocation now for her to leap at Katie again.

It was hard to concentrate on her friends though. She realized she needed to get a very good idea of where she was, and quickly at that, before nightfall turned everything the same shade of black. This knowledge would help her in future, if they managed to get away from here.

So, while Runt and Katie quietly discussed something by the truck's hood, and Six-Six ogled her breasts, Heather looked around and tried to commit everything she saw to memory.

The most obvious thing was that they were now high up a mountainside; and yes, just a few steps away there *was* a house waiting for them to enter it.

Heather didn't pay the house too much attention for the moment though.

What else is there around here? she pondered.

This clearing where they'd stopped wasn't at the top of the mountain, it was rather an abrupt outcropping of rock that formed an incomplete cliff, incomplete because the drop existed only on the side opposite the house. The clearing was almost like a mountain road that went nowhere; once past this wide expanse where Katie had parked, it quickly narrowed again and then abruptly fell away into thick woods through which, if one looked down the mountain slope, one could see the twilight-gray waters of a river.

In the distance, Heather could see wide expanses of cultivated farmland, a beautiful tapestry of alternating shades of green based on what crops each plot contained. All the farms were so far away however that she wondered how high up they actually were, and also if they were still in Massachusetts at all. Judging from the amount of time that Katie had been driving, they could just as easily be somewhere in Vermont or even New York State now.

"No phones, no GPS. Heather, we're in big trouble," Danni whispered in her ear just as Runt and Katie finished their discussion and walked towards them.

Danni had wiped her eyes dry and seemed more composed. Heather glanced at Maude. Maude scowled back at her, as if blaming her for their current straits. "Damn fuckwits," she growled under her breath, staring at Runt with a particularly evil eye. The wound on her forehead had dried now, but the blood from it extended like a stripe of war paint down her left cheek to her left breast, where it seemed to have glued her blue tee shirt to the bra beneath it.

"We'll find a way to escape," Heather whispered to Danni. She gave Maude a smile, trying to build camaraderie and perk her spirits up. Maude didn't seem to give a shit, however. She seemed locked in her rage; angered further by her inability to express her intense frustrations.

Six-Six gave Maude a rough shove that almost flung her to the ground.

"Hey, watch it!" she growled at him as she straightened up again.

"Alright, girls, let's go into the house," the giant said, with that loony smile plastered on his face again.

From his general behavior, Heather fixed Six-Six's mental age at about seven; meaning that all this might seem like a kind of game to him: joining his more mentally normal brother and sister in a game of kidnapping young woman for . . . for what?

Well there's certain to be forced sex involved, that's for sure. They're going to rape the three of us. But what comes AFTER they've had their way with us, is what REALLY worries me.

Chilling news stories about the grisly fates of abducted female hitchhikers tormented her mind; broken and rotting bodies found in shallow roadside graves. Would the three of them wind up like that?

No, no no! She shook the thoughts from her mind. *I won't accept that. I simply can't.*

"And remember," Runt added with an ugly grin, "any attempts from any of you to escape and that person'll get a face full of buckshot."

Katie sneered at Maude. "Try being sexy after that, slut. Try giving some guy head when you've got no head."

"That's really cute," Maude spat right back. "You're quite the monster, Katie, you know that?"

Heather studied the house as they were herded towards it, their feet trampling the crisp and wet grass. It was a large log cabin, with a roof of dark wooden shingles, wooden slat windows, and it appeared to have been caulked with ancient clay. It was built right up against the mountain, inserted as it were into a natural cleft in the rising rock face, so that the stone mountainside apparently formed both its rear and right-side walls. An old oak grew by its left wall, the giant tree's fan of leafy boughs completely shielding the house from aerial view.

Also invisible now—perfectly blended in with the lush tree foliage—was Katie's army-green pickup truck.

The building's apparent age really bothered Heather. From its design it looked to have been built in the seventeenth century, despite which it was in good condition; as if the seventeenth century had ended just yesterday.

"This is a museum relic," Danni mumbled to herself. "It ought to have rotted away at least two hundred years ago."

"This is not somewhere I wanna be right now," Maude said.

No it isn't, Heather agreed as they stepped up onto the wide porch. *And Danni's right too—this log building reeks of authenticity—so how is it still standing after all this time?*

The porch was clean of dirt and had an ancient rocking chair sitting on its right side. At their approach, two salamanders ran sideways off the porch and vanished into the grass.

So, from the looks of it, this cabin has been sitting here like forever; up here in the middle of nowhere. But if that's so, how did Katie and her brothers happen on it? No, not just her brothers. They mentioned another woman . . . Electra . . . another sister or a female cousin. What the heck? Does their whole family live up here too? Oh, my God, what have we gotten into?

And then they were walking past Katie, who was holding the door open for them, into the centuries-old house.

CHAPTER 8

Abandon Hope, All Ye . . .

The log cabin's interior was sparsely furnished with rough-hewn furniture—pine chairs and an oak dining set. Half-consumed candles hung in dusty sconces on the walls.

The three captives weren't granted the luxury of looking around, however. Almost as soon as they'd entered the front room, they were herded out of its far end and down a short hallway. But not before Heather had been able to note that this house they were walking through didn't seem to be in much use. Yes, it was well-maintained, but when she'd looked into the kitchen, she hadn't seen any cooking pots or utensils in there. Nor did the two bedrooms on either side of the hallway seem lived-in either.

This keeps getting stranger, she thought, growing yet more disturbed. She looked back once towards the living room and tried to see around Six-Six's monster silhouette. Outside, night had completely fallen. She wasn't certain what the time was now, but thought it had to be about 9 p.m.

Maude was the foremost of the three captive girls, following Katie and Runt who were leading the way, illuminated by Katie's cellphone flashlight. Runt had just turned into the third and final room along the hallway, ahead on their left. Maude slowed her pace till she was abreast with Danni and Heather.

"Hey, it doesn't look like anyone actually lives in this place," Maude whispered in a very worried voice.

"This building is just a front," Danni whispered back. She still looked scared, but now her geek/nerd mind had sliced a path through her fear. Heather had already deduced as much from her comments on the log cabin's age.

"A what?" Maude asked.

But before Danni could explain, Katie turned back to them. She stepped aside from that final rear doorway and gestured at them with her revolver. "Alright, inside and downstairs. And don't you dare make a fuss."

Downstairs?

But Heather's question was answered quickly enough. Once through the indicated door, they found themselves faced with a large trapdoor in the floor of the last room. Beyond the trapdoor a wooden bed stood by a window. The floor was tiled with rectangular stone slabs, four of which had been removed and placed upright against the wall. Against the nearer of the bed's legs lay the rolled up end of the bearskin rug it stood on. Once the stone tiles had been replaced and the rug rolled down again, there would be no way to tell that a secret room or passage lay below the house.

The trapdoor had wooden stairs leading down from it and Runt was already down there in the half-darkness, where a single candle sputtered in the sconce beside his head. He peered up through the opening and waved the barrel of his shotgun at them. "Alright, girls, down here, one at a time. And no tricks."

Heather went first. As she descended those steps, she was well aware that her options were fast reducing. She'd gotten a good mental picture of the house, but that would be useless if they were going to be locked away in the depths of the mountain.

Her concerns made her steps falter and she stumbled the last quarter of the way down the stairs. Her momentum carried her into Runt's side.

To her surprise he didn't shove her off.

She looked down at him. It was strange to her, being able to look down at an adult man—but that was how short he was. The ugly man was grinning up at her, baring those dirty teeth.

And if she had any doubts as to why, a moment later she felt Runt's hands grasping her buttocks and squeezing, pulling them apart. He laughed. "Oh yeah, you feel real good to me, honey. This ass of yours is as soft as a burger bun."

A huge desire to spit in his face filled her. But scared of what the consequences of her doing so might be, Heather instead tore herself away from him and started up the ladder again. But Danni was coming down it now and there was no way around her. Heather hung there, wanting to flee, but unable to go anywhere. Meanwhile, she could hear Katie growling at Danni to "Move your fat ass before I shoot it off!"

The impasse was revolved by Runt grabbing Heather around the waist and physically lifting her off the ladder and putting her on the ground. She squirmed in his grasp and once his hands were off of her, moved well away from him, which meant heading down the tunnel they were standing in. She stopped after about ten yards and waited for Danni and Maude to catch up with her, by which time Runt had walked past the three of them and was gesturing with his hand that they follow him.

"See what I meant?" Danni whispered on reaching Heather. "That old cabin outside was simply a front. Downstairs . . . here inside the mountain is where Katie's family actually lives. I'm sure they leave that cabin unoccupied."

"Yeah," Maude instantly agreed. "So they can trap unwary travelers who fall asleep up there."

"The worrying question is," Danni said in a trembling voice, "what the hell do they want with us three?"

"Think 'rape' and you can hardly go wrong," Maude spat. Blood was dribbling down her face again; while descending the stairs she'd banged her head on something and reopened the wound in her forehead. Scowling, she added, "The way that piece-of-shit called Six-Six keeps grabbing his crotch at me, I'm . . . but if he touches me, I'm going to kick his balls off!"

"Calm down, Maude," Heather whispered, pushing the others ahead of her. "Getting mad won't help us in this situation."

"I can't help it. This is just so wrong. And to think that someone I thought of as a sister did this to us."

"Yes, yes. But right now we need to think up a plan of escape."

The tunnel led downward in a gentle slope. Someone had doused the candle by the trapdoor; now they found their way using the light from Katie's phone, which, projecting from behind them, threw their shadows forward like black ghosts. The tunnel walls were smooth gray stone and seemed unworked by tools.

"This is the entrance to a natural cave," Danni explained as they went on. "It'll soon expand into—"

"Shut up and keep moving," Katie growled from behind them.

Heather could already smell food cooking up ahead. She realized that Danni's deduction that they were about reaching some kind of wider space was correct.

By now the tunnel was lighting up again. About a minute after noticing this brightening, the tunnel ended in a large cave.

"Wow!" Danni yelped on seeing where they'd been brought.

The house upstairs had been odd in its anachronism. This cave however . . .

The cave was oblong in shape, about thirty yards long and ten yards across. It was about the height of a normal room in a house. They'd entered at one end; a second tunnel exited at the other. The cave had three dark wooden doors set in its left-side wall.

A large amount of furniture was set around the cave, forming a time-travel mixture. Some of the tables and chairs seemed to have been made at the same time as the log cabin upstairs was built, while other furnishing, like the foldable steel chairs and plastic tables in evidence, might have been purchased yesterday from Walmart or Kohl's.

A few feet away from them, on their left as one entered the cave, a cage had been built against the wall. The cage was six feet high and eight feet long, and made from wood and metal pipes and chicken wire. Inside it were a couple of old blankets on the floor and a pillow or two.

"Oh shit!" Heather gasped on seeing it. Her fear stemmed not so much from the sight of the creepy enclosure, but from the fact that the cage's floor and wooden posts were stained with blood.

"What was that?" Danni asked. "What did you just say?"

"Oh, just the nasty smell of this place," Heather lied. At this point she was spatially the leftmost of the three of them, and thus the position of her body prevented her friends from really noticing the cage. Fearing the outcome of her revelations, she decided against telling Danni and Maude what she'd seen. Thankfully, both of them had either not noticed the cage or had glossed over it due to more worrying concerns. They'd discover the bloody enclosure in their own good time.

"Yeah, it really stinks in here," Maude said, wrinkling her nose in disgust. "Of cooking meat and pee and bucketloads of sweat."

"Yes, and there's another unpleasant smell too," Danni added, looking like she was about to vomit. "Something bad unlike anything I've ever smelt before in my life."

Meanwhile both young women were looking further down the cave. Heather tried to forget the bloody wire cage. She instead forced her attention onto what her fellow captives where staring at. Which honestly wasn't much better.

"Oh my God, what are those for?" Danni asked, pointing in horror at the rows of hooks affixed to the nearest of several wooden beams that ran crosswise across the cave ceiling at four-yard intervals, and which seemed meant to brace up its ceiling against a cave-in. The hooks dangled on rusty steel chains nailed to the underside of the beams. Additional hooks and chains hung from several of the wooden uprights that kept the beams in place across the low ceiling.

"I really don't wanna know the answer to that question," Maude said, her eyes widening like saucers. "Shit, shit shit! We're in deep shit!"

"Keep moving to the center of the cave," Runt said, shoving Heather and Danni in the back. Heather didn't like the fact that they were being pushed towards the dangling hooks. In the meantime Katie seemed to have vanished through the first of the cave's side doors.

As they went forward, more details came into view. Heather now saw the source of the cooking smell she'd begun perceiving out in the tunnel and which here in the cave was almost a fact of life:

In the cave's center a large cauldron sat on a metal tripod and bubbled over a blazing wood fire. This fire was built in a shallow pit, beside which stood several steel drums and a sturdy oak worktable on which lay lots of gleaming knives and other kitchen implements. Beyond the fire, several cords of wood were stacked against the cave's right wall. The smoke from the fire ascended up into a funnel-like metal chimney attached to the nearest overhead beam. From the chimney's end, a thick aluminum pipe extended across the ceiling and exited the cave through its farther entrance.

This central fire was one source of light in the cave, but a number of rechargeable electric lanterns also hung on the walls, meaning the family either had a gasoline generator or solar panels hidden up in the old wood cabin, or they were somehow charging the lamps from the pickup truck.

"Alright, stop right there," Runt said when they were directly under the hooks.

They froze trembling. The significance of where they were standing wasn't lost on them.

"Take your clothes off," Six-Six said with a lascivious leer on his lips. "All a them."

Danni gaped at them. "Oh no—I'm not stripping naked in front of—"

Six-Six punched her in the mouth. Danni's head instantly snapped back. She staggered on her feet and would have fallen over backwards had not Maude quickly grabbed her. When Maude got Danni standing upright again, Danni's lower lip was split wide open and her mouth was dripping blood. In addition, one of her lower incisors seemed to be loose. Danni stood reeling on her feet with her eyes crossed.

Maude scowled at Six-Six. "You didn't need to do that, you bastard."

The giant laughed and flexed his huge fingers in her face. "Get undressed, bitch. Or you'll get some too."

Heather was already slipping her tee shirt off, after which her bra quickly followed, and then her jeans and underpants. Finally she kicked her flip-flops away. *Keep calm,* she told herself as Six-Six's eyes roved up and down over her nude figure, *just keep calm. Panicking won't achieve anything here. Keep calm and plan how to get us out of this mess.*

Maude was almost naked too; she was hastily sliding her shorts down her legs.

Danni was still swaying on her feet though, fumbling with her tee shirt but seemingly too stunned to figure out what to do with it. She'd make a motion of sliding the tee shirt up over her breasts, then seem to forget that this was what she intended doing and drop her hands again.

Runt began laughing. "Dammit, Six-Six! Kid, you don't know your own strength. You've damn near knocked the girl out. She's so groggy now she can't even undress herself."

"I'll help her get nekkid," Six-Six said and pulled a long black survival knife out of a sheath strapped to his thigh.

Heather gasped in fright as he stepped towards Danni, but all he did was grab her tee shirt in one hand and slice it open down the front with the other. Then he dug his hands under the waistband of her pants, and after fondling her private parts for a while, slit her pants and panties open also. A few more expert cuts, and pants and panties both made a slow trip down Danni's wobbling legs to her ankles.

Six-Six grabbed a feel of Danni's breasts and then he and Runt walked round the three girls. Heather held Danni upright as the men appraised them.

"What you think, bro? Runt asked.

"Yeah, real delicious-looking," Six-Six replied. " 'Specially this one"—he fondled Heather's buttocks—"Oh, I can't wait to eat her."

Eat me? No, he doesn't mean it like that, does he? Heather wondered in confusion, the alternate meaning of the word too sinister and scary to believe. *He just means eat my pussy; as in performing cunnilingus on me. Yes, of course, that's all he means. We're just going to be raped and held prisoner here for years, right? Not . . . no, it can't be that. That's impossible. No one does things like that!*

Okay, so yes, Heather and her two naked friends *were* facing the bubbling cauldron and the giant worktable as the brothers walked around them fondling them and making brutish comments about their physical assets, but there was nothing to indicate that anything more sinister than being sexually assaulted was in store for them—as if being raped wasn't horrible enough already. She could tell the cook was making a soup—and it actually smelt nice—but . . . but . . . She couldn't shake off the alarm that had suddenly overtaken her.

She looked at Maude, to see if Maude shared her unease. But Maude was in a world of her own. Runt was currently fondling Maude, and she was doing her utmost best not to scratch at him while he slipped his fingers into her vagina. Heather found herself squirming in empathy with her friend's humiliation.

Six-Six grabbed Maude's hands and raised them over her head so that she was helpless to stop the investigation of her private parts. Maude howled when Runt forced her buttocks apart and slipped two fat fingers up her anus.

"Stop it, please!" she shrieked in pain. "I'll do anything you want. Just stop it, please!"

"Aw, girl, stop pretending you don't like what I'm doing to your ass. You're real slack back here, like your asshole's seen a whole lot of cock. Hell, I'm sure Katie could park her Ford truck in your backside without difficulty."

"A Ford truck up her ass! Yeah, that's a good joke," Six-Six chortled. "Hahahahaha! Yeah, a great joke!"

Maude cringed at the statements and her face reddened both from embarrassment and from additional anger. Whatever calm she'd been managing to maintain was visibly evaporating fast.

Heather looked away, staring instead at the 'kitchen' worktable, with its array of long knives. She considered the possibility of her dashing to the table and grabbing one of those knives and stabbing Runt and his giant brother with it.

If I'm going to do it though, it has to be now or never. Once Katie comes back . . . I can't take on all three of them. And there was the problem that she was still holding onto Danni. *How do I put her down without either of them noticing? Maybe I should just shove her at them and make a run for the knives and grab two at once. But if I do that, I'll have alerted them to my intentions and I can't face off against their shotguns. No, I have to use stealth here.*

But she'd delayed too long thinking. Her opportunity for action had already passed. As if they'd realized they were being lax, Runt and Six-Six had stopped humiliating Maude. Six-Six let go of her hands and she instantly covered her breasts with them.

Runt wiped his shitty fingers across Maude's lips and then scowled at his younger brother. "Where the hell're Katie and Electra? What's keepin' 'em both?"

"I'll go get 'em," Six-Six said happily and set off across the cave towards the first door in the wall.

Heather watched him go, thinking that here might be her chance to grab a knife and disarm this asshole Runt; maybe with Maude's help. Maude, spitting copiously and endlessly wiping her lips, looked like she'd murder Runt if she could just get the shotgun away from him.

Oh heck! She's gonna blow up soon for sure and then . . .

She didn't blame her friend for her anger though. Right now, Heather agreed that Maude had justifiable cause for her rage.

And me? So far, I've been lucky and no one's hurt or molested me. But that won't last long. Not with that cretin Six-Six saying he'll love to eat me!

She turned her attention to the table again. Could she do it? Six-Six had vanished through the door he'd left for. Runt was standing beside Maude; but though his shotgun was pointed towards them, he wasn't paying much attention to them.

Yes, I think I can make it. Heather started lowering Danni to the ground, but then her attention was caught by a strange smell. Just like Danni had earlier mentioned, it was a smell unlike anything she'd ever smelt before. And just like that, her curiosity over the origin of this unfamiliar and nauseatingly unpleasant odor truncated her escape attempt.

What on earth is that awful stench? From Danni's earlier comment, it must have been present in the cave all along, only she'd not noticed it over the smell of the cooking meat. Even now it was difficult to perceive, but it was there, like the stubborn lingering smell of a fart after a room has been deodorized. The smell was coming from the direction of the farther exit, of that Heather was certain.

She peered that way, trying to work out what it was that reeked so outrageously. It smelt like rotting . . . oh, but she really had no reference point, nothing that she could honestly liken it to. All she knew was that it stank hideously.

"That's one godawful smell," Danni said then. "Like a shit took a shit and then that shit took a shit of its own."

Heather looked at her. "Yeah, but what the hell is it?"

Danni's eyes had uncrossed themselves now and her legs had regained their strength. She leaned away from Heather and wiped the blood from her mouth with the back of her hand. "That bastard hit me," she whispered, feeling inside her mouth and wobbling one of her front teeth. "Goddamn braces tore my lip open."

"Danni, what do you think that smell is? It comes and goes, but what is it?"

Danni kept feeling her wounded mouth. "I've no frigging idea."

"Well, you sure took your sweet time," Runt suddenly said, to the sound of approaching footsteps.

Oh, dammit! Once more Heather realized that her chance to take an action to help their circumstances had passed. She turned and saw Katie returning with several lengths of rope in her hand. Heather wasn't too surprised that the ropes appeared bloodstained.

"Where's Electra?" Runt asked as Katie reached them. Katie had changed her clothes; in addition to being barefoot, now all she had on were a pair of cutoff denim shorts and a blue bikini top. Heather assumed this was due to the heat in the cave. The cave was warm, but not too warm. And also, a draft was coming from somewhere, most likely from the farther entrance, and circulating an internal breeze, so that the air smelt fresh despite the cooking going on.

Katie shrugged. "Electra? Oh, she's getting dressed. She was playing with Pet when I got there. Six-Six is with her now."

Runt handed Katie his shotgun. "You watch 'em. I'll tie their hands."

Katie pointed to the blood on Danni's face. "They give you any trouble?"

"She didn't get undressed fast enough, so Six-Six gave her a little love tap."

Katie laughed.

"You're gonna pay for this, you Judas bitch," Maude sneered at her. "You'll get what's coming to you for sure."

"Yeah?" Katie laughed louder. "Only in your erotic fantasies, slut."

"Hands out," Runt told Maude. Still scowling at Katie, Maude stuck out her hands. Runt quickly bound them together with a length of cord. Once this was done, he raised her hands up over her head and, pulling her up momentarily onto the tips of her toes, hung her wrists over a steel hook.

"Well now we know what they're for," Danni told Heather before sticking out her own hands and getting the same treatment.

The hooks over their heads were set at varying heights and these heights had clearly been carefully calculated. Once all three girls' hands were hung above them, the soles of their feet comfortably touched the floor, but the strain on their arms was the same despite the difference in their statures. The overhead chains were also supple enough that they could turn around in all directions.

"This just gets worse and worse," Danni whispered to Heather. "I wonder what the hell is next."

"I think all that remains now is for us to meet Electra, the bitch responsible for all this," Maude growled, huddling close to the others.

Heather really wished Maude would keep her temper under control. Making cracks like this was certain to do them no good. If Runt heard her . . .

"Hey, Electra's coming," Katie said then.

Runt looked up. "Yeah. Finally, we can get this party underway."

Heather and her two friends turned and had their first sight of Electra.

CHAPTER 9

Electra

The woman approaching was younger than Heather, Danni and Maude. She was at most 19-years-old. Like Katie she was dressed in faded cutoff denim shorts and a dirty bikini top. Her long black hair dangled down over her breasts. Her skin was impossibly white, as if she'd never once been out in the sunlight. Her eyes were as black as night, as impossibly dark as her skin was pale.

Electra was tall and slim and very beautiful. Heather found her beauty very creepy.

Electra was accompanied by something like a dog with a human face. At first Heather didn't understand what she was looking at, but then she realized it was a deformed teenager of about fourteen years old, running about on all fours like a hound. The teenager loped around Electra like he was an actual canine pet, licking at her hands and nuzzling her buttocks with his nose. His arms were very long, and his legs very short and crooked, making moving about on all fours his easiest means of locomotion. His body was completely hairless and he was also completely naked, with his genitals dangling between his thighs like a tail.

When the doglike teen looked at Heather, his eyes revealed a lack of intelligence that made Six-Six seem like a Nobel Prize winner. She shivered and felt very cold.

"Down, down, Pet!" Electra scolded the deformed boy with a loud smack to the back of his neck. "Go play with Katie."

The dog-teen barked twice and hurried over to Katie's side and began sniffing her crotch. She pushed him away with a look in her eyes that was part amusement and part fondness.

Heather shivered some more. *What the hell is going on here?*

Electra stopped in front of Heather. "I'm Electra Hemingway," she introduced herself, a statement which revealed her perfect pearly-white teeth. Unlike the two brothers, she seemed to have some regard for her personal hygiene.

She smelled really bad though. Heather quickly identified the pale woman's body odor as the same horrible one that kept occasionally sneaking its way through the aroma of steaming meat. The only problem was that Electra had come from the wrong direction. Except if the room she'd emerged from looped around to connect with the exit behind them, the real cause of the smell was still unknown.

"I'm Heather," Heather said. "And my friends are Danni and Maude. Please let us go. We don't mean you guys any harm. And we can't even lead the police to you. We don't even know where we are at the moment."

Electra lifted a hand and stroked Heather's face. In marked contrast to the perfection of the rest of her young body, her fingernails and toenails were all long, dirty and cracked. They were yellowed like an old crone's and their broken tips cut Heather's soft cheek.

Electra laughed. "I'm afraid you can't leave here." Her voice was calm and pleasant in the sort of way that a graveyard was sometimes an oasis of serenity.

"Hell no, you girls ain't going anywhere ever again," Runt said. "This is sorta like that song . . ." Then he scratched his head, looked as confused as Six-Six usually did, and stared at his sister for help: "You know, the one dad likes so much?"

"Oh, you mean *Mama's Pain Dungeon* by Slain Jane," Katie said. She laughed over Electra's shoulder at the three captive girls and with the deformed dog-teen prancing around her like a dancing ape, she began singing:

"Honey, you can get in,
But you can't ever get out.
No point pleading, bitch,
We warned you what we're all about.
Lean back, try to relax,
We're just gonna pluck one of your eyes out,
And, hey, we're just getting started,
It's gonna be quite a fun party . . ."

"Yeah," Runt said, "this is just like that. You girls are fucked but good, and we ain't even begun fucking you yet. Ha ha ha!"

Danni instantly began crying again. "Oh my God, why can't you just leave us alone?"

"Na na na na na na!" Katie mocked her. "Oh, what a crybaby! Na na na na na na! Just wait a little while. Then you'll really have something to cry about!"

"Leave her alone, you damn bully!" Maude raged at Katie. True, with their hands hung up over their heads like this, she was helpless, but that didn't mean she couldn't kick. She kicked violently at Katie, who quickly stepped back and out of her way.

"Okay, enough, all of you," Electra Hemingway said, which instantly resulted in silence and made Heather wonder what strange power she held over the three siblings.

"Who are you?" she asked Electra.

"What a silly question to ask at a time like this," Maude spat at Heather, her red hair whirling about her head as she angrily turned to face her. "She's clearly their creepy little sister!"

Electra smiled at the statement. "No, I'm not their creepy little sister," she replied Maude, grinning broadly with a brilliant display of her perfect teeth. "I'm their creepy mother."

Heather's eyes opened wide at the statement.

Danni's did too. "Their mother?" she asked. "How can you be their mother? You don't look a day over twenty!"

Electra laughed. "Actually I'm three hundred and forty-six years old."

"But that's impossible!" Danni insisted. "No one can live that long." She stared inquisitively at Katie. "No . . . no."

Katie shrugged. "Yeah, she's our mom alright. And she's telling you the truth about how old she is."

Danni looked back at Electra. "But how? How?"

"There are secrets, arcane ways to accomplish whatever you set your mind to do. Anyway, my children call me 'Electra' and not 'mother' because, like you pointed out, I look younger than all three of them." She extended a pale hand backward, with her fingers extended and her looped and broken fingernails spread like claws ripping open the fabric of time and space. She laughed. "They're all jealous of me, of course; especially Katie. But I've promised to teach them the secret too, once they're old enough to handle it wisely."

"How is this possible?" Danni asked, her nerd-intellect once more getting the better of her fear.

Electra Hemingway leaned closer to Danni, making the girl flinch from her unpleasant smell. "Those secrets I mentioned permit it to be. Of course, I won't share them with you, but you'll share in them in me."

"What the hell are you saying?" Maude said, finally finding her voice. "And I think you're lying. You're not three-hundred and whatever. You're just some bratty YA wannabe."

"What's YA?" Electra Hemingway asked in some confusion.

"It's a marketing category," Danni enlightened her in a trembling voice. "Kids between the ages of thirteen and nineteen. In essence, YA—or 'young adult'—is another word for 'teenagers,' but it's one that makes them feel self-important and makes them spend their pocket money or earnings on products designed and targeted specifically at their age group. This cooperate marketing ploy is a raging success, of course."

Maude rolled her eyes at Danni's fear-induced and long-winded explanation. "You nerdy idiot. She already knows that. Look at her. She's not some 300-year-old grandma relic! She's probably eighteen herself and plans on holding us for ransom so she can have enough money to buy a fresh bookshelf of paranormal romances. Use your brains, nerd. Who the fuck in this day and age names their daughter Electra, of all things? The stupid, dumb—"

"Maude, calm down," Heather said. She was very bothered by Electra Hemingway's crazy assertions, but even more bothered by the way that the woman (dammit, could she actually be telling the truth?) was smiling placidly at Maude's rant.

"So . . . what do you want with us three then?" Heather asked.

"My family and I are going to eat you all," Electra replied simply. While all the captives gaped at her in shock, she added, "A long time ago, I discovered during my supernatural research that human flesh is the one true ambrosia, the food of the gods that keeps one eternally young. And you can see the evidence in my body now."

The moment of awestruck disbelief passed. Heather realized she had to believe her ears. Six-Six hadn't been joking earlier. He'd meant what he'd said: he and his crazy family really did intend to consume them as food. Heather didn't believe Electra's rant about any supernatural benefits of eating human flesh, but that wasn't the point.

The point was that Electra clearly believed it; and so did her 'children' (a word which also had cultist connotations). Katie was licking her lips now. As was Six-Six, who'd rejoined them and was once more squeezing his crotch while ogling all the naked and restrained female flesh on display. Six-Six had also changed his clothes: now all he had on was a dirty white jockstrap that bulged and throbbed as if he'd stuffed a live anaconda inside it.

Heather saw Six-Six staring at her and quickly looked away. She felt sickened to her stomach. She could practically read all the evil and disgusting thoughts in the giant's mind. She prayed that she'd die before he got his filthy hands on her.

And that just might happen, she realized, returning her mind to the clear and present dilemma facing them.

"You're gonna *eat* us?" Danni was asking, her eyes so wide, they seemed stapled open. "You're gonna frigging *eat* us? But you *can't* do that."

"Yes, we can," Runt said. "And, yes, we will."

Danni was adamant in her rebuttal: "No, you just can't do something like that. You can't kill and eat people to live forever. Even religions don't demand that anymore. You just cannot do it to us."

When Danni mentioned 'religion' all their captors burst out laughing.

"Religion, little girl? What do you know of true religion?" Electra Hemingway said, laughing in their faces. "I think your religion tells you to eat your God to remember that *we* killed him. My religion however asks me to eat *you* to live forever."

And this—this statement of Electra's—was what finally made Maude lose it for real:

"Goddamn crazy religious-fanatic psycho-bitch!" Maude said.

"What did you just call me?" Electra grabbed hold of Maude's chin with both hands, her horribly long and yellow fingernails stabbing into Maude's cheeks and drawing blood.

The look of intense anger in Electra's jet-black eyes, the merciless smile on her beautiful face, and the frigid tone of her graveyard-wind voice, should have alerted Maude to her peril. At that moment Electra Hemingway even seemed to *smell* different. These changes definitely warned Heather and Danni though, both of whom instantly withdrew into themselves, with both young women subconsciously packing away all of their self-defeating belligerence into a shell of harmless timidity, and leaving not even the barest impression of a protest concerning their predicted fates hovering on the surface of their personas.

Maude, however, was too far gone; too angry to perceive danger. "I said you're crazy! You're nuttier than chipmunk poo-poo! Goddamn cannibal bitch!"

Electra frowned. "I won't be mocked by my food."

And then, essentially because that was exactly what Maude would do under conditions that made no sense to her, Maude spat in Electra Hemingway's face. It was a lot of spit too, as if Maude had been pooling it up in her mouth ever since they'd arrived here in the mountainside cave.

The gooey sputum hit Electra in the eyes and dripped down her face and around her lips, down her chin and fell thickly onto her small breasts.

Oh shit, now she's gone and done it, Heather thought in terror. At that moment she felt a spiraling dread swirl up around her. The horror seemed to rise from her feet and pierce her brain with hooks. The only way that Heather could conceive of herself not now witnessing something that would indelibly traumatize her was for the ground to open up right away and swallow her whole.

Otherwise . . .

And then Electra Hemingway smiled. She ignored the spit dripping down her preternaturally youthful face. Instead, she raised a hand and snapped her fingers. "I feel thirsty," she said, the smile on her face widening. "I really need something to drink."

"Mom's thirsty," Runt said, his voice coming from somewhere behind Heather. "Hold on, I'll get the knife and the glass." She heard him moving behind her and then the sound of his picking objects off the table beyond the fireplace.

Oh no! Heather thought. She turned desperately to Maude. "Listen, just apologize. Say you're sorry for spitting on her. Just say you're sorry!"

"Fuck you too!" Maude said with a defiant stare. "I'm goddamn *not* sorry." She shook her arms, trying to dislodge them from the hook securing them overhead, trying to lunge forward and reach Electra. "I'd kick her bratty teenaged ass to pieces if I wasn't hung up like this!"

Heather turned to Electra. "Look, she didn't mean it! She honestly didn't mean it!"

"I know she didn't," Electra said, with that same creepy smile on her face. "That's why I'm no longer angry with her."

"You're not?" Heather felt some relief. She glared at Maude, who pointedly looked away from her as though she felt her apologizing on her behalf was a betrayal.

Maude was still scowling at the cave wall when Electra Hemingway stuck the knife that Runt had brought her into the side of her neck.

Maude, her arms and hands hung above her, was helpless to halt the deadly penetration. She jerked taut when the blade pierced her throat, then gave a yelp of pain as Electra jiggled the knife about a little, severing both the carotid artery and jugular vein on that side.

By the time that Maude realized what was happening to her, her blood was already squirting out of her neck in thick red jets, with Electra Hemingway expertly collecting it in the glass goblet that Runt had handed to her along with the knife.

"Wha . . . wha . . . !" was all Maude could gasp while dying, her green eyes gaping in shock.

Once she'd half-filled her goblet with Maude's blood, Electra got out of the way of the red jets and let them squirt onto Danni and Heather instead.

Danni instantly began screaming hysterically.

Fuck this! Heather thought and began screaming too as Maude's blood arced through the air and splattered them both. She tried to get away from the crimson drenching, but the hook she was hung on wasn't about giving way either.

She gaped open-mouthed at Electra, expecting her to drink the cup of blood.

But Electra didn't do this. Instead, after Katie helped her slip her bikini top off, Electra Hemingway moved the goblet to her shoulders and began pouring Maude's blood over her chest. As if she was helping her apply suntan lotion, Katie smeared the blood all over Electra's naked torso, cupping her hands around her mother's breasts and pinching their nipples so that they stiffened.

Still screaming along with Danni, Heather looked around at the rest of Electra's psychotic family. Six-Six and Runt were both laughing at them, chortling and slapping their sides as if Maude's murder was the funniest thing they'd ever seen in their fucked-up lives. Even the dog-teen Pet was laughing too, barking and rolling over on his back and kicking up his legs in his excitement, just like a real dog would do.

Then Pet got back onto his feet and shuffled forward and began licking the blood dripping down Maude's side. While doing so, the deformed canine kid frisked restlessly back and forth, once even leaping up to nip at Maude's nipples. Maude was dead now, staring somewhere inside her head with only the whites of her eyes visible, unable to rage at this added humiliation.

Meanwhile, Electra moaned with pleasure and spilled more blood on her breasts in a thick line as though she were a human cake applying red icing sugar to herself. Katie smeared the blood lower and lower, rolling her hands in slow circles, her fingers making round grooves in the red mess, working her way down around Electra's navel and under the waistband of her shorts.

"Oh yes, child!" Electra Hemingway gasped. "This feels so good."

Oh, God Almighty, I'm in Hell, Heather thought then, as the sights and the demented laughter threatened to drive her crazy. *I'm still alive, but I'm in Hell.*

For her part, Danni had already fainted.

And there was worse yet to come. Because from this point onward, sanity seemed to go on its summer vacation.

CHAPTER 10

Chop My Bitch Up

"I'm sorry to disappoint you," Electra said once the goblet of blood was empty, "but we aren't vampires. It's human flesh that has the magical power to keep me young and beautiful, not blood." She posed proudly before Heather, drenched from the neck downwards in Maude's blood, and with her torso now designed in almost aboriginal red spirals by Katie's fingers. Her nipples were erect, big tips on small breasts, but now her voice betrayed very little sexual arousal.

Katie, meanwhile, did appear to be sexually aroused; as did Six-Six, who was grabbing her ass and drooling, though she afterwards shoved him away with a look of amusement on her face.

"No, we ain't vampires," Runt agreed, accepting the bloody cup from his mother and walking out of view again, shortly after which Heather heard him clank it down on the table behind her. "We only eat human flesh."

Heather had no idea what to feel. Of course, she was used to the concept of murder—it was everywhere, all you had to do was turn on the TV and the latest death tolls hit you in the face like a bullet, so much so that after a while your soul became bulletproof—but this was the first time she'd ever seen someone actually get killed.

But to be killed in such a horrible way—slaughtered like one of ISIS's American captives?

Oh, my God! Oh, my God! Oh, Maude!

The shock of what had just happened threatened to unnerve Heather, but she was a tough young woman and she fought to maintain her sanity. Heather knew that if she cracked up now, she and Danni were both finished.

She glanced sideways at Danni. Danni hung limp, her body swaying at the ends of her arms. She tried to avoid looking at Maude's corpse. Pet was now nosing between the cheeks of Maude's buttocks, seeking for turds freed by her passing.

Heather returned her attention to Electra Hemingway.

Electra now had her back to them and was having a conversation with her 'children.'

Heather still couldn't understand how this teenager could be mother to not one but three adults—but she'd decided that to preserve her sanity, she needed to go with the flow. On witnessing Maude's brutal death, Heather had fast realized that she had two options here: She could either remain in a state of denial (which wouldn't help her), or she could accept whatever she saw and was told by these crazy people at face value. She understood that the latter option might not help her either, but . . . it would at least prevent her mind from imploding. It didn't matter if *she* believed their insane stories; what mattered was that Electra Hemingway and her family believed them; and whether delusional or not, they were acting based on these beliefs.

Electra was speaking to the others. Heather listened:

"It was unfortunate that she was so stupid," Electra said. "The three of them would have provided us with sufficient meat for at least a couple of months. But now we'll have to cook her early."

"You haven't commended me for finding them, mother," Katie said, pouting petulantly.

Electra stroked Katie's cheek fondly. "Of course, darling. You did an excellent job and of course I'm very proud of you." She glanced back at the three girls. "It'll be nice to have some juicy and tender meat for a change, and not all those tough, stringy fishermen that your brothers catch in the woods."

Runt shrugged. "Aw, mom, it ain't our fault that women hardly ever go fishing."

Electra nodded. "I know, darling. That's one area I really think the feminist movements need to address. I'm not blaming either you or your brother. But it's nice to have a change in our diet, you understand."

Runt nodded. "Yeah, mom, we know what you mean."

A memory seemed to flash in Six-Six's dull mind. His blue eyes lit up like he was thinking hard and then he said, "Hey, Electra, we did bring home that woman and kid two months ago. Those were nice 'n' juicy."

"Hey, yeah, that's right we did," Runt agreed.

"And the Gutter'd gotten to 'em first too. Gutter saved us the trouble of guttin' 'em both ourselves."

"Yes, you're right," Electra quickly agreed, then added, "The son was great—juicy and tender and delicious. His mother though . . . oh, the old bird was almost as tough as our regular diet of fisherman."

Heather had been listening intently. If she'd been able to view her emotions logically and as separate from herself, she'd have been surprised at how, each time she imagined she'd seen the worst, this 'worst' was almost instantly one-upped by something even nastier. In this case, what she found worse than Maude's death and the fate intended for she and Danni, was the idea that this had been going on for a long time.

They've been murdering and eating people up here in the mountains for years? And no one knows?

But then Katie asked a question: "Hey, Electra, what's this 'Gutter' thing the boys keep talkin' about? I asked Runt 'bout it on our drive up, but he said to ask you instead."

Electra Hemingway sighed and looked really annoyed. She sat on a chair and stared at Katie. "The damned Gutter? I still can't believe that it got away."

"Got away?"

Electra nodded. "Yes. I summoned it up from the abyss as a sort of cleanup service. You know how Runt is always complaining about the charnel room starting to overflow with bones and human waste and how bad the stink is and all that?"

Katie nodded, her nose wrinkling up. "Yeah, the charnel room stinks so bad, I almost puke each time I walk past it. So?"

"Well, my idea when I summoned the Gutter was to have it eat up all the bits of folks that we weren't going to throw in the stewpot. Sort of the way Toilet cleans up our poop and keeps the place clean for us."

"Yeah?" Now Katie looked slightly angry. "So, what happened?"

Electra sighed again. "Well, first of all, it turned out that the Gutter only liked fresh guts, not the old decayed stuff we've got in the charnel room; it wouldn't touch the corpses. Which only partially helped our problem. But before I could send it back to the Abyss, Six-Six fucked it and it escaped."

Katie's anger was instantly replaced by confusion. She looked up at Six-Six. "You fucked a demon?"

The dumb giant grinned dreamily. "Don't blame me, sis. I thought it was you. You offered me a blowjob and I said yes. It was a great blowjob too."

"Huh?"

Electra explained. "That's the problem. The Gutter is a shapeshifter. It can take on any form it pleases, down to the minutest detail. Anyway, after *satisfying* your brother"—here she rolled her eyes—"it took the other exit out of the cave." She pointed to the farther tunnel. "And so it's been haunting the woods for the past two-and-a-half months, killing folks for its meals. It's extremely dangerous, Katie."

Heather listened quietly. Her arms both ached from being raised over her head for so long, but she refused to let the pain distract her. She forced herself to concentrate on what her captors were saying. She wasn't sure how this information about the Gutter could be of any use to her, but she absorbed everything she heard; she felt that her survival depended on remembering everything that was said.

Beside her, Danni had begun mumbling to herself, seemingly having a nightmare but unable to wake up from it.

So that's the thing we saw run across the highway. Yes, and now, thinking back Heather realized that when the 'Gutter' had first walked out from the trees it had looked like a smaller version of Six-Six. *But if it's that dangerous, why didn't it attack us?*

Runt's next words provided that explanation:

"We've tried to catch it so that Electra can return it home," he said, "but the damn thing's as cunning as a werewolf. It never changes from its human form if it thinks it's in danger."

"Otherwise, pa says we can just shoot it and have done with it," Six-Six added. "Pa says that killing the Gutter'll definitely send it back to Hell's pits. But we can't go around shooting folks in case we go shoot some state cops and start an manhunt for us."

"And according to your father," Electra said, "it can read minds to some degree." She sighed loudly.

"Dad said that?" Katie asked. "But can't he dispose of it himself?"

"It's outside the range of your father's magical abilities, honey," Electra said, still looking upset. "He's tried hard, but he can't ever seem to manage it. So the Gutter is out there now in the Massachusetts woods, making a complete nuisance of itself and we've no way of getting it back up here. We're hoping the police accidentally shoot it for us."

Katie looked across the cave, towards the final door before the tunnel exit. "Dad can't deal with it? Wow, that's a first."

So, I know now that there's at least two more of them, Heather acknowledged, looking back over her shoulder. *Their father, who seems to be asleep in that last room over there, and someone or something called 'Toilet,' who's their janitor . . . though Katie seems to dislike that description. Or maybe she just dislikes 'Toilet' himself. And, if Toilet is anything like Pet, I can see why.*

The malformed Pet was still nosing Maude's anus and every now and then trying to stick his tongue up inside it.

"You can discuss the Gutter with your father later," Electra told Katie. "Maybe both of you can come up with a way to catch it, or at least find and kill it before it creates real problems for us." Then she pointed over to the captive girls. "But for now, we need to cook our fresh kill before it starts getting spoilt."

"Yeah, alright," Katie agreed. "But I'm famished. Can't we eat first?"

Electra shook her head. "Not till it's done. Otherwise you'll all fall asleep afterward and *I'll* have to cut her up."

"And Six-Six'll be too horny by then to do any work," Runt added, pointing to his younger brother's prodigiously bulging crotch.

"Yeah, yeah, let's do it," Katie sighed. She walked away from them towards the 'kitchen' worktable.

Runt also left the others, but went the opposite way, towards the first door.

Heather pretended not to notice Katie as she went past. She was both disgusted and terrified of Katie. She was also very wary of making the same mistake that Maude had, of letting her anger and revulsion get the better of her. From what Electra had said, the family intended keeping she and Danni alive for a while yet, possibly for several weeks even; but not if they made a nuisance of themselves.

Heather made a mental note to point this out to Danni once she returned from her nightmare.

Katie had meanwhile returned from her trip to the oak worktable. She was carrying a wide plastic basin, like something one would bathe a child or a dog in. After shooing Pet away from licking Maude's anus, Katie positioned the basin under Maude's corpse. To do this, she had to lift Maude up and put her legs into the bowl.

"Alright, she's ready for you," she said once she'd gotten Maude properly arranged.

Runt reappeared then, naked except for black underpants and a bloodstained apron. In his right hand he held a foot-long knife. He grinned at Heather. "You'd better take a good look at what happens to her. Same thing's gonna happen to you too real soon, baby."

Heather tried to look away but couldn't. She tried to close her eyes, but they seemed determined to stay open. She felt as though her soul had taken her prisoner and was forcing her to view what was going to happen next.

With a wide grin on his ugly face, Runt dug his knife into Maude's belly, just below her sternum. He seemed to take deep satisfaction from ripping the shiny blade down to her crotch. Then he pulled the bleeding sides of the tear open and let her intestines spill out of her and hang down over her thighs.

Heather had once watched a sheep being disemboweled on a TV documentary. The sheep corpse had been hanging upside-down from a hook; and because of this, when it was opened up, its guts had poured down over its head. The butcher in the documentary had been expert at wielding his knives, turning the dead animal into cuts of meat with a speed and a precision that had amazed Heather. She'd been surprised at how something familiar and warm and living could so quickly become something else, merely a commodity that was displayed on a counter and purchased for one's nourishment. When the butcher was done, the sheep had been annihilated—from what remained of it on the chopping block, it was impossible to form a mental picture of anything other than food, as if the act of separating it into strips and chunks of mutton had automatically erased (and forbidden) any human memories of the cuddly living object it had once been.

In essence, the expertise that had accomplished the sheep's deconstruction had legitimized its purchase for human consumption.

Runt was displaying similar finesse now, reaching inside Maude's dangling body and cutting away at the ligaments that held her viscera in place. After some quick slicing, the sound of which made Heather almost wet herself, Maude's entire mass of intestines dropped out of her body and fell into the basin around her feet.

"Too bad that the Gutter got away," Electra said, walking over to stand behind Runt and placing her hands on his shoulders. "It would have loved all this tripe." As Runt dug his knife into Maude's left thigh and began sawing a thick cut of meat away from the bone, Electra called out, "Hey, Six-Six, don't just stand there like an idiot, son! Bring over that plastic pail, so we can separate the useless parts of her from what goes in the stewpot."

The way she'd said it, as if Heather's dead friend was of no more consequence than the sheep she'd watched getting butchered in that farm documentary, twisted Heather's heart in a dark rage. But the disgusting smell of raw flesh and draining blood was getting to her too.

Unable to control herself, she began puking. The vomit kept coming and she kept throwing up, unable to stop herself and not even trying to.

Electra looked over at her. Then she dispassionately snapped her fingers. "Hey, Pet! Over here, boy!"

A moment later the deformed teenager was crouched around Heather's feet and eating up her vomit.

"Yeah, that's a good doggie," Electra said, bending down and scratching Pet behind the ears. Then, seeming to forget about Heather altogether, she returned her attention to Runt's work. Directing traffic as it were, Electra Hemingway began pointing out to Six-Six which parts of Maude's guts were to be disposed of: "No, no, son, you should know by now that we don't want the gall bladder in our stew!"

Runt had meanwhile peeled all of the flesh off of Maude's left thigh and had begun work on the right one. Once again, he worked with the sort of efficiency that meant he'd been doing this for a long time, possibly for years. His forearms were both as covered in blood as Heather was in vomit. For her own part, Electra was painted bloody anyway.

Heather began crying. No, she didn't want to cry; she wanted to continue to be strong and to defy their captors. But even though they hadn't yet broken her will and she was determined to keep fighting against these outrages she was being subjected to, something suddenly gave way inside of her and she found herself unable to stop the torrent of tears that burst from her eyes.

So she wept, wept long and bitterly. She wept for Maude, wept for herself, and wept for Danni too, who was still locked in her dream realm and seemed scared to wake up to experience the real nightmare happening to them.

Her captors of course ignored her tears and concentrated on cutting Maude up.

CHAPTER 11

Hank & Jory

Once Hank Rollins had gotten the kid out to the riverside, he began making proper preparations—baiting the trap as it were.

The first thing, of course, was to work out how to set things up.

Hank had already figured out that he needed to sit with his back to a tree; that way the monster couldn't sneak up on him from behind. He'd also noticed that the thing seemed to go for one's belly. So to forestall having his own guts pulled out, Hank had 'armor-plated' himself: under his hunting jacket he'd buckled a broad aluminum plate across his belly. The plate was originally an aluminum stock pot that he'd sliced up and hammered flat.

Oh, I'm ready for that murdering sonofabitch, Hank thought.

While holding Jory by his left arm, Hank first looked out over the silently flowing river, then up at the sky.

The moon wasn't yet out, so the night was dark. The mountains across the river formed brooding shapes. Hank hoped there would be a moon tonight. He'd brought along two flashlights, but he didn't want to use them except he needed to. He didn't want the monster to suspect that he was after it. He wanted the damned thing to feel safe. He wanted it to suspect nothing up until the moment when he blew its damn head off. Once he'd set up everything the way he wanted it, he intended to duct tape one of the flashlights to the barrel of his shotgun. That way he'd have no problem with both seeing and shooting the creature at the same time.

He roughly shoved Jory towards one of the trees. Hank didn't enjoy being so hard on the kid, but Jory didn't seem particularly smart; the kid seemed unable to understand what was expected of him. *Has to be all that beer I gave him earlier to calm him down. Anyhow, what else was I supposed to do? Otherwise the boy would be completely unmanageable.*

Yeah, this tree will do, he decided, picking out one that was slightly separate from the others. It wasn't too thick, so he could easily rope Jory to it, and more important, there weren't any trees between it and the one he'd chosen for himself, so he'd have an unobstructed view of it.

As expected, Jory wasn't very cooperative when Hank told him to lean back against the tree, so Hank slapped him in the face.

The slap seemed to wake Jory up somewhat. After that he protested less. He couldn't really protest anyway, since Hank had him gagged with duct tape, but his body language became more cooperative, like he was now willing to die for Hank's cause.

So Hank pushed Jory against the tree. Then he shone one of his flashlights in the boy's face.

"Stand there and don't move," Hank sternly warned him. "I need to sit down by that tree back there and calculate my trajectories so I don't blow your head off. And, I'm warning you for the first and last time now: don't you dare get any silly ideas about running off."

Hank kept the light shining in Jory's face until the kid realized that he was supposed to nod that "Yes" he understood what Hank was saying. Then, still not trusting Jory not to try and make a run for it if he turned his back on him, Hank kept his eyes on the kid and backed off towards the tree he'd chosen for his vantage point.

Maybe I should have tied the boy up right away. But I first need to make certain that I won't be aiming at him. It's a bit unwise though, leaving him unbound to the tree like this. But then, how far away can he get, even if he does make a break for it?

So Hank retreated until he'd reached his own selected tree. One reason why he'd chosen this particular tree was because it had a lot of high grasses growing around it, which made for great concealment. Hank sat down, picked up his shotgun and trained it at Jory's tree.

The kid just stood there. He was looking in Hank's direction now, knowing where he was in the darkness because of the flashlight that Hank was holding up beside the shotgun barrel. He was making no attempt to get away. Which was great. Apparently, the boy had realized that his elderly captor had the right idea and had decided to simply play his part in this hunting drama and collect his paycheck afterwards.

Or maybe, he'd simply given up hope, realized he might die here tonight, and decided 'the hell with it.'

Either way, he wasn't making a run for it, and that was all that mattered to Hank. Hank sighted carefully along the shotgun barrel, playing the flashlight across Jory and then off into the woods on either side of him.

Yes, I can easily hit it from here; no problem at this range. I just need to keep alert so that I get it before it gets near Jory . . . once it reaches him I'll have to use the hunting knife instead. . . . So firing from here and aiming away from him . . . well, I can't aim at him anyway, that would be cold-blooded murder! Or maybe, once I see the monster coming, I'll sneak forward and shoot it at almost point-blank range. . . . Alright, time to tie the kid up and let's start our waiting. This may be a long night for both of us.

Hank leaned his shotgun against the tree and then, after making certain it wouldn't fall over, picked up a roll of duct tape and stepped out from the cluster of tall grasses.

Playing his flashlight beam across the dark ground, he quickly crossed the riverbank to Jory's side again.

"Alright, son, now let's get you properly tied up. Just remember, try not to wet yourself when the creature appears. I'm not going to shoot you, so just calm down, and once this is over we can both return to our daily lives." Jory nodded and Hank relaxed. Thank God, the boy was finally seeing this his way. He continued speaking to put Jory at ease: "Listen, the way I see it, we've got until about midnight before this thing shows up, so—"

Then suddenly, Jory moved. Hank gaped in surprise as the kid's knee caught him in the balls. The pain that shot up through Hank's crotch at the impact was better imagined than described. Yelping in pain, Hank just managed to stay on his feet. Realizing that his mission for tonight was in jeopardy, he reached out to grab Jory before he ran off.

But then he discovered that Jory had been faking him. The kid pulled out his hands from behind his back and Hank saw that his hands were now untied.

But how? How did he . . . ?

And then, before Hank could either grab the kid or defend himself, Jory jerked him forward by his hunting jacket. For a few seconds Hank had the weirdest thought—that this kid he'd abducted was gay and wanted to kiss him—but next thing, Jory's knee connected with his crotch again.

"Shit!" Hank howled, and this time he did topple over, grabbing his testicles as they throbbed in pain. Sure, Hank had protected his belly with that hammered-out aluminum plate, but he'd never expected he'd need to make a metal codpiece too!

The kid stood over him for a few seconds, then he bent down and picked up Hank's dropped flashlight and ran off between the trees.

"Come back here, you little punk!" Hank growled hoarsely as Jory fled off into the darkness, his path of departure marked by a strip of yellow light. "Come back here right now!"

But of course the kid paid him no attention, and in a short while Hank was left alone in the darkness, nursing his aching balls as he lay there on the ground with the river gurgling just a few yards away.

CHAPTER 12

A Whole Lotta Meat

By the time Danni woke up from her faint, Runt had finished butchering Maude.

After Danni groggily opened her eyes, she stared at the basin of meat and blood next to her in some confusion, being at first unable to connect the pile of raw red flesh to Maude's death. She'd forgotten why she'd passed out.

Then Danni's gaze snagged on the two sets of leg bones projecting out of the meat pile, and like a salmon being reeled up through the water towards its fatal rendezvous with the fisherman, she found herself unable to stop following the progression of peeled bones higher and higher. The more horrified she grew as Maude's stripped skeleton was revealed to her gaze, the more of it she had to see, as if her terror needed this ultimate verification.

Heather watched her warily. Heather already felt totally traumatized. At first, she'd tried looking away from the butchers. She'd stared instead at her feet, and then later turned and looked towards the far exit. But the cutting and hacking noises and the back-and-forth motions around her, and most of all the crazy conversation beside her—crazy because its very normalcy signified the madness of its speakers—had kept drawing Heather's attention back to what was going on right next to her; to what apparently would later be her own grisly fate also:

"Quite a lot of fat on her. Nice fatty breasts . . . makes good oil."

"Wow, what a delicious-looking liver she has! We should make some pâté out of it."

"Electra, we really need to figure out how to get a freezer up here."

"Trucking it up here's easy enough. The electricity is the problem."

"I'm gonna discuss this with dad."

"Alright, Katie. Discuss our food preservation troubles with your father if you insist, but until you two come up with something better that actually works, I'm just going to keep my stewpot bubbling. This method's worked fine for me for over three centuries and I'm not about changing it just because you children want to keep up with the times. In this case the old ways *are* best. The food tastes sweeter, and it's more nutritious, with a fine blending of old and new—"

"Hey, Electra—we're almost out of spices! We've barely a pinch of thyme left!"

"Tell that to your sister! Katie was supposed to get us a fresh batch of spices from the supermarket where she works."

"I did, mom. I really did . . . but I forgot 'em. They're all back in Raynham."

"Where you can't ever return to now, 'cos if you do everyone's gonna wonder where your three friends vanished to, right? Li'l sister, sometimes you act so dumb I mistake Six-Six for Einstein."

"Shut up, dwarf. Just drop the damn lungs in the bucket with the tripe so I can throw them in the charnel room!"

"Hey, I'm not a dwarf! Don't you dare call me that!"

"WHATEVER, DWARF!"

"Hey, Pet, stop humping that pussy. Here, boy, bring it back right now! You dare spurt come on those fine buttocks and I'll whip your doggy ass! Those are *food*—I've been looking forward to eating that tight ass ever since I first set eyes on the girl. Hey, Katie, tell that li'l piece of shit to bring that meat back here right now."

"Pet ain't a piece of shit! Don't you dare call him that."

"Li'l sis, if your Pet don't bring those buttocks back here right now, he's gonna look like a piece of shit when I get done whipping his ass with my damn belt!"

"Pet, Pet, here here, come here, boy. Don't mind grumpy Uncle Runt. He don't want you to fuck like we adults do. Alright, kid, let's have the asshole back. That's a good doggie!"

"Hey, Sprint, you lobotomized her, hahaha!"

"Six-Six, cutting off a person's butt ain't lobotomizing 'em. It's 'lo-bo-tomize,' not 'lo-butthole-mize.' "

"What's the difference?"

"Argh—jest forgit it! Kid, sometimes you make Pet look like Einstein."

"Hey—leave Pet out of it!"

"Katie, make Pet hand over that damn ass before I do!"

"Hey, Electra, who's Einstein?"

"Some guy who wrote a book about relatives, son."

"Relatives. Oh, I get it—Einstein's a marriage counsellor, just like that guy we cooked six months ago."

"No, I think he helped us win World War Two, son."

"Hey, Runt, here's the damn buttocks. And see what you've done now? You've gotten Pet all upset! He's crying."

"For fuck's sake, feed the mutt some puke, wilya! Punch your friend over there in the gut so she throws up again."

"Stop that right now! And you just want that ass back so you fuck it yourself. I'll be watching the pot to make sure you actually do cook Maude's buttocks. You damn perv!"

"Aw, shut up, slut."

"Perv! Perv! Hey, Pet, Uncle Runt's a perv!"

"Children, children, please! Let's get this done with and have our dinner."

"Yes, please, please, mother. I'm so hungry I could eat Runt's brains. Not like he has much of those 'cept in his dick."

"Aw, fuck you, slut."

"You'd love that, wouldn't you? Well, forget it, you ain't having none of this hot bod and tight pussy. And for God's sake, man, frigging hurry up with severing those lungs! I ain't got all night to wait for ya."

All of this was uttered in the drollest way imaginable, without even the vaguest of suggestions that anything out of the ordinary was occurring. None of the arguments were really mean-spirited; it was just edgy conversation to pass the time. The cannibal family actually sounded like stand-up comedians acting out a sketch. Even the doglike teen Pet was soon up and about again, scampering excitedly to and fro the cave, investigating smells and once even cocking his leg and peeing against one of the cave's support pillars.

They sound just like my mom and my sisters do while preparing dinner, Heather thought. *So normal that it's abnormal.* Heather's family had a dog too, which made the similarity all the more disturbing; except that Graf was housebroken.

And while the raillery and chatting went on, more bits and pieces of Maude were stripped away. Her heart was sliced out, chopped up and skewered onto a metal spit, along with both of her kidneys and her tongue. This spit was then placed on a kebab stand and set to roast over the blazing fire.

Maude's stomach was severed at both throat and duodenum ends, then split open and emptied of its contents, after which her lungs finally did end up in the bucket containing her guts.

These lesser tasks were handled by Six-Six. While bantering with his mother and sister, Runt had ruthlessly reduced Maude to a mere framework of bloody bones.

It was amidst all of this that Danni woke up and saw what remained of her friend . . .

Danni screamed at the sight that greeted her. Maude's head—her tongue-less mouth gaping open in a grimace of teeth, her bloody arm bones rising beside her ears, up to her hands, which being secured at the wrists, both still had all their flesh.

"Oh, she's awake," Katie noted on returning from dumping the tripe.

"Yes," Electra agreed with a frown. "She's really very loud. I preferred her asleep."

Her scream exhausted, Danni slumped against Heather.

"Just try to keep calm," Heather whispered to Danni. "We'll get out of this nightmare somehow. We *will* escape. We won't die like her."

Danni buried her head between Heather's breasts. By now Heather's arms really ached from the lack of blood flow and she could hardly feel her hands at all. All she could do was keep her mind strong.

And hopefully keep Danni strong too. Though I've no idea how long either of us will last if horrible things like this continue happening tonight.

***

"I think we're about done now," Runt said, getting to his feet and stretching. "Alright, Six-Six, take her legs out of the basin and carry the meat over to the stewpot. I'll go throw the skeleton in the pit."

"No, no," Katie said quickly. "Remember that Pet likes the hands and feet." She frowned at Runt. "It's the least you can do after depriving him of Maude's ass."

Runt nodded. "Alright, Six-Six, break off her hands and feet for Pet. And then—"

"Hey, darling," Electra called out to her son, while rising from the chair she'd sat on all this while, "I want her brains too."

Runt nodded again. Once Six-Six had snapped both of Maude's feet away from her ankles, which with the giant's immense strength took mere seconds, Runt unhooked her skeleton and dragged it off to the worktable.

Electra crossed the cave to a large upright cupboard. "Now that you kids are finished, I'll start serving dinner."

Runt lay Maude's skeleton out on the worktable and picked up a meat cleaver. Two cleaver strikes later and Maude's hands lay separated from her body. He waved the severed hands at Pet (who leapt up and down barking excitedly), laughed and said, "See, Uncle Runt ain't such a bad guy after all," and then picked up a saw and began sawing off the top of Maude's head.

Danni had made the mistake of peeking that way. Now she began crying again. She once more buried her head between Heather's breasts and wept and wept.

"Hey, stop that!" Runt growled at Six-Six just before he emptied the bowl of raw meat into the steaming cauldron. Then he slapped Six-Six hard across the face. The slap was so hard that Heather was certain Six-Six was going to react angrily, but no, the moronic giant just looked confused; not as if he'd been dazed by the blow, but because he clearly had no idea what he'd done wrong. And so Runt enlightened him:

"When the hell are you ever gonna learn? Six-Six, you don't pour the raw flesh into the pot until *after* Electra's served us our dinner. Then it can cook all night long and we can have some of it with our breakfast. You do it the other way and it's gonna mix up with the cooked stuff and make everything uneatable."

"Uh, sorry," the giant said. "I won't forget again."

Katie laughed. "That's what you said the last twenty times." She'd walked over behind her brothers and was now leaning between them with her hands up on both of their shoulders. "Hey, Runt, go easy on the kid, huh? It's been a long day for us all."

Runt just 'Hmmphd' and resumed scooping out Maude's brains.

"Oh yes, we are gonna get out of this frigging madhouse somehow," Heather mumbled to herself, while wishing she could faint so she didn't have to witness any more of this craziness.

CHAPTER 13

Hank

It took Hank Rollins eight minutes to recover enough to stand up again.

Hank knew that during boxing matches, if a fighter got hit by a low blow he was allowed a five minute respite. Never having been hit in the testicles before, Hank hadn't really understood why the rest period had to be so long.

But now he certainly did. Being kneed in the nuts once was no joke . . . but twice?

"When I catch that young punk, I'll . . ."

With the help of the tree Jory had been standing beside, Hank pulled himself up to his feet. He leaned against the tree, holding his crotch and hoping he hadn't been permanently damaged down there. That was how it felt—like his balls had been knocked right up into his belly.

He'd have liked to sit down beside the tree till he felt fully recovered. But he was conscious that Jory had been running away all this while and with a ten-minute head start, who knew where the kid had gotten to now. Maybe he'd reached the highway and was flagging down help. Or was even alerting the police to his kidnapping.

Hank frowned at that latter possibility. *I'd better start looking for the little sonofabitch and when I get him, I'll . . .*

Taking careful steps, he crossed the riverside clearing to the tree against which he'd propped his shotgun. The moon was out somewhere now, which was good, because Jory had taken Hank's flashlight with him, and until Hank got the other one out of his knapsack, he needed to be careful where he placed his feet.

Hank reached the tree. He got his extra flashlight out of his knapsack, picked up his shotgun, and then, still walking gingerly, he set off into the woods after Jory.

CHAPTER 14

Dinner

"Dinner is served," Electra Hemingway chirped brightly.

"Finally," Katie said, rolling her eyes. "I was starting to think we weren't eating tonight."

The family's dinner was stewed human flesh, with brown bread and red wine.

Electra, behaving like mothers everywhere—and this was when Heather finally realized that the nineteen-ish teenager was in fact really an old woman, and a *really* old one at that—had bustled about getting trays and dishes and cutlery out from several cabinets and laying places for five on a table near the cave's middle side-door. She'd even put on an apron and looked the very image of 'kitchen pretty.' The only things spoiling this picture of domesticity were the length of her horrible nails (Electra's toenails in particular were a jaundiced yellow and so curved and crooked that they made it look like she had some incurable foot disease), the blood still splashed all over her, and the fact that what she pulled out of the bubbling stewpot for her family to eat were human body parts—chopped up arms and legs, and large anonymous cuts of meat that could have come from any portion of the human anatomy.

"Hey, Runt," she called, waving those nasty fingernails at him, "come and take your father his dinner."

Runt wheeled over a short wooden cart with a large steel basin on it. Electra heaped cooked flesh into the basin. Runt wheeled the cart away to the cave's furthest door, knocked on it, and after a short wait, pushed it open and entered. The door shut behind him, but not before Heather had recognized an abrupt increase in that unidentifiable and horrible smell.

Oh, so it's their dad who stinks like that. No wonder Electra smells that way too. And why doesn't the family patriarch come out and eat his dinner with his cannibal brood? Only one sensible answer to that—their father must be an invalid; which may also account for the smell . . . it's a symptom of his illness. And judging from the amount of food that Runt just wheeled into his room, their father is quite an obese invalid.

The smell of the cooked human meat was revoltingly appetizing. Heather felt her stomach roiling, but also found herself salivating. After all the vomiting she'd done she was suddenly hungry.

Without waiting for Runt's return, the rest of the family arranged themselves around the table. Electra sat at the head and Katie on her right, facing the wall. Next to Katie a place was set for Runt, with a steaming pile of meat awaiting his return. Six-Six had the other side of the dining table entirely to himself. Six-Six also had more food than anyone else. His tray was heaped with miscellaneous cuts of human flesh, atop which lay an entire arm, minus the hand.

The final table place, at the end of the table opposite Electra, was set with an empty plate. Heather assumed this honorary place was for the family's sick patriarch.

Pet the dog-boy was sitting on the floor with a juicy boiled foot clamped between his jaws. He ate exactly like a real dog would, savagely ripping the meat from the bone with his misshapen teeth and wolfing it down, then gnawing on the bones gripped between his stubby fingers.

Electra smiled at her son and daughter and they all began eating.

"Hey, Six-Six, don't hog all the bread," Katie soon said.

"Except for that mutant kid, this seems so fucking normal that I was almost expecting them to say grace first," Danni whispered to Heather.

Heather nodded back. Danni's eyes were red from crying, but she seemed to have gotten her courage back. Which was good, because courage was what they needed right now.

"I know," she replied. "And we have to start looking for their weaknesses. Anything we can use against them. They'll let us down from these ropes sooner or later and then we'll have a chance to make a break for it."

Danni looked up at the rusty hook holding Heather's hands suspended over her head. "Heather, my arms are killing me. How much longer do you think they'll keep us like this?"

Heather first tried to shrug, but couldn't with her arms raised, so she shook her head instead. "I'm not sure. But I think that sooner or later, they'll lock us in that cage over there." She found it strange, how she was able to ignore the cannibals feeding right next to them. (And apparently Danni could too.) "If they don't, we'll both complain that we need to use the bathroom. That's certain to work. I don't think they'll want us shitting so near their kitchen."

Danni nodded and looked over towards the cage. Heather felt relieved now that she'd not earlier mentioned the cage's bloodstains to Danni and Maude.

Danni looked away from the cage and turned back to stare at Katie's feeding family. Runt hadn't yet returned and Katie was making a joke: "This sure tastes better than livin' on burgers and hot dogs," she said. "You've no idea how hungry I kept gettin' while rooming with those three dumb bitches."

Danni grimaced at the insult. "If we do make it away from here alive," she whispered to Heather, "before we leave, I want to really hurt these sickos if I can. I want to break Katie's neck and maybe also stick one of Maude's feet up her ass."

Heather managed a grin. Yes, she needed Danni exactly the way she was now—scared but ready to rumble. Amped up with the right kind of adrenalin, with her 'fight or flight' reflex ticking away like a time bomb in the 'fight' zone.

Because, hands-down, Danni was the smartest of the four of them.

Maude had had a temper and could be really gutsy once riled up, but her reliability had always been hit-or-miss.

Katie had proven herself to have cunning and to be a great schemer—despite her hatred of Katie now, Heather had to admit that Katie had played them all like a mistressmind, infiltrating their friendship for almost four months, and all just so that she could feed them to her crazy family.

Me, I'm calmer than the others. I don't know why I'm calmer, I should be frightened out of my wits, but I'm not. Maybe it's a delayed reaction. But calmness alone won't get us out of here. Danni is the nerd—she's the one with the brains here and for us to escape I need to get her to stop thinking about her own peril and to start analyzing this crazy situation for its weak points—everything has an Achilles' heel.

Heather had always been realistic about her own limitations and her friends' strengths. So now, she understood that she was locked in a symbiotic relationship with Danni. She needed to keep Danni's spirits up so that the girl could think for both of them. If there was a way out of this mess they were in, Danni would locate it; Heather had no doubts whatsoever on that score.

Runt reappeared then, alerting the girls to his presence by slamming the cave door behind him. Heather once more smelt that underlying foulness as the door shut, and then the aroma of human broth smothered it again.

At her son's reemergence, Electra Hemingway looked up from chewing on a rib. "Did your father enjoy his meal, dear?"

"Yeah, he sure did. Said to tell you you're the best cook in the whole damn universe."

Electra grinned. "Of course I am. That's one reason why our marriage is such a happy one."

Six-Six looked up from tearing a chunk of meat off the arm on his tray. "Hell yeah, Electra. Ain't nobody can cook people like you do!"

Electra resumed eating. Runt pushed the cart against the wall, its meat basin now empty again. Before joining his family at the dinner table, he walked over to their captives.

Heather tried not to flinch at the dwarf's evil stare. Hairy as an ape, and with his muscles bulging everywhere now that he'd discarded his bloody apron and was dressed in just his underpants, Runt was squeezing his crotch as he stared up at them both and was clearly enjoying their discomfort.

Ironically, one of Heather's main problems with Runt was his height. It seemed more acceptable to her to have the giant Six-Six abuse her, rather that this muscular midget who hardly reached the height of her ears, notwithstanding that he was wide enough to make two of her from.

Runt's ugly lips curled up into an ugly smile. "No food for you two girls tonight. We're gonna wait till you're both starving before we feed you. That way, you won't start putting on airs 'bout being too good to eat what we eat and start puking it back up."

"Or spitting it in our faces," Katie laughed from the table, lifting her wine glass to make her point. "Warn them 'bout doing that, big bro!"

"Yeah," Runt said nastily. "A guy did that to me once. Imagined he was a tough guy and spat some meat back in my face." He leaned forward and licked Heather's cheek. "Know what I did to him? I cut off his dick and ate it for breakfast. Roast dick tastes real good; like bacon, but tenderer. Then we made kebabs of his nuts and fed them to Pet."

"We don't have dicks, dickhead," Danni said. "Or nuts either, you nutcase!"

Runt grabbed both of her breasts and squeezed them hard, his large hands completely covering them. "True, but you've got these, haven't you, mouthy missy? Titties make great roasts too, don't'cha know? Add a little stubborn tongue on the skewer and maybe you won't have so much to say anymore, wilya?"

"Yeow!" Danni looked like she'd resume crying, but she toughed it out.

Runt let go of her breasts. Red fingermarks decorated them now. "Screw you two bitches. Just don't spit on us and you'll live longer before ya die."

"I am so going to castrate that rape-culture dwarf," Danni whispered as Runt joined the others at the table and began eating.

"Hey, we need to use the bathroom!" Heather called out.

Electra scowled and pointed a six-inch-long cracked index fingernail at her. "Young woman, if you ever again make another statement about using the toilet during our family meals, you're going straight into the stewpot. There's a time and a place for everything and I won't have you ruining my appetite with potty conversation. Have I made myself perfectly clear?"

Heather nodded quickly. "Yes, yes. I'm really sorry."

The rest of the family's cannibal dinner passed in an uneasy stalemate between captives and captors.

There was one positive though: Heather noticed that Danni's eyes had begun gleaming in that questing way they had of doing when she was thinking really hard about something. And from the way her eyes were darting everywhere around the cave now, it was clear that Danni was thinking about their escape.

Heather resolved to keep silent and not distract her.

CHAPTER 15

Hank

The first place where Hank went to look for Jory was at his Jeep. Not because he thought the kid could have driven his Jeep away—the keys to the vehicle were still in Hank's pocket—but because of the $10,000 stashed in the Jeep's glove compartment. The kid might have stolen the cash.

This wasn't the case though. The forest around the Jeep Cherokee was as silent as Hank had earlier left it. Hank walked round the black Jeep for a while, playing his flashlight over its windows and peeking into its interior. Then he got down on his hands and knees and shone the flashlight beam under the vehicle. No, the kid wasn't hiding there either.

But if he didn't come back this way, then where could he have headed to?

This question again brought the worry that Jory might have gotten away to the highway and flagged down help. Dammit, the kid might right now be blabbing to the police about his abduction. Which would put Hank in a whole lot of trouble with the law.

Hank's groin still ached, so he climbed up on the Jeep's hood and sat there to rest for a bit. He did some quick thinking: *Where the hell did that stupid young punk run off to? I need to catch the monster and I need human bait to catch it. So I need to find Jory again and quickly at that. Aw . . . shit!*

Hank had just realized that him leaving his flashlight on was a very silly thing to do. *Jory can see it! And once he does . . . that'll mean that he knows exactly where I am! Damn! He may even be looking at me right now from the trees and I wouldn't know.*

He was about to snap the flashlight off, but then changed his mind, deciding instead to practice some cunning himself.

So what Hank did was, he got down off the Jeep's hood and opened the driver's door and pretended to root through its interior, shining his flashlight over the backseat as if he'd lost something in there. Once he was certain that Jory—if he was watching—would be satisfied that he wasn't looking for him, Hank took the $10,000 out of the glove compartment and put it in one of the pockets of his hunting jacket. That done, he locked the Jeep again and after shining his flashlight at the surrounding trees, stalked off into the woods, muttering, "Now where has that damn kid gotten to," loud enough for Jory to hear him if he was close by.

Hank kept the flashlight on until he'd once more reached the riverbank. Then he snapped it off again and went and stood by the water. Shotgun crooked in his right elbow, he waited there by the water's edge for a long while, his mind replaying him the grisly images of his son Hank Jr.'s corpse as it had lain torn and dead at this exact spot in the shadow of Misery Mountain; Junior, with his stomach ripped open by that horrible thing and with his head underwater, his lips blowing bubbles like a damn fish and . . .

A fish splashed and made the surface of the water ripple. Hank jerked out of his mental haze of pain and turned back towards the woods. Slowly, with his heart heavy, but with fresh determination to see this thing through, he stepped in amidst the trees again.

He had to find Jory, and he'd just figured out a very simple way to go about doing so: Now that his own flashlight was turned off, he simply had to wait for Jory to switch *his* flashlight on, and then grab him again.

You can run, son, but you can't get away from me, Hank thought with a cold smile, stepping carefully now to avoid making any noise. *I'm going to catch you again. Have no doubts about that!*

CHAPTER 16

Sex and Violence

The cannibals had been drinking a lot during their appalling dinner.

Heather hadn't failed to notice their gestures towards she and Danni. It wasn't hard to speculate what was going through their perverse minds, particularly not when Runt, while chewing on a strip of someone's skin, made obscene gestures at them, and when Katie began fellating an empty wine bottle.

Heather expected the worst—that it was almost Rape Time.

Oh no, here we go! she thought nervously as the family, all a little shaky now after sharing three bottles of red wine between them, began getting to their feet.

"We'll just leave the plates here, for you two slaves to wash up in the morning," Runt said, looking at Heather.

"And where are we supposed to get the water to do that?" Danni asked.

Heather thought Danni's question a strange one, as she could easily make out the five industrial drums ranged around the cooking fire; and there were two others beyond the stacked cords of wood. Surely those had water in them.

But then she understood that Danni had her reasons for asking: she was clearly just fishing for information while the entire family were slightly drunk and less on their guard than earlier.

Six-Six pointed towards the cave's far exit. "You'll fetch water from the river, girls . . . hehehe! Usually that's my job; but seein' as you'se both livin' here now, you'll be doin' it."

Heather saw a spark of satisfaction enter Danni's eyes at this answer. *Yes, that's what she wanted to know.*

That question had been Danni's first statement since she'd begun her meditation. She lapsed back into her rumination. Not for long though.

Trouble was already on its way over.

"Alright, girls, time for a li'l sex," Runt said, shambling over to them.

Danni instantly emerged from her reflective reverie. "You're going to rape us?"

Runt leered at her. "Sure, why not? I'd've thought you'd be gagging for it anyway. Li'l sis says you were headin' outa the state to see your ex for sex! Ha ha ha!"

Danni shot Katie a look full of hatred.

Katie was picking her teeth with a shard of finger bone. She had turned her dinner chair around to face the captives and was sitting with her left foot folded up on her right thigh. She paused in cleaning her teeth, spat on the floor, and then shrugged at Danni. "Yeah, it's true, Runt. She was draggin' us all outa the state just to go get fucked by some scumbag." She scowled at Danni. "Bitch, if you don't stop giving me that damn evil eye, I'll go get my mom's whip and come peel all the skin off your fat ass with it."

Electra laughed. "You'll love my whip, Danni. It's a cat-o'-nine-tails and has sharp pieces of glass tied into its knots that are intended to tear your skin to shreds." She too had swiveled her chair to face her sons and the captives, and was sitting in the exact same pose as her daughter—left foot up on right thigh—which, Heather figured, meant that Katie had subconsciously learnt it from her. This position also gave Heather a distressingly clear view of Electra's horrible toenails, which were as long and confusedly curved as a cloverleaf flyover with multiple levels and as yellow and dirty as if they belonged to an ancient corpse. Looking from the cannibal matriarch's beautiful teenaged face and her fantastic body to the revolting tips of her hands and feet, Heather found it impossible to unify these two divergent aspects of Electra Hemingway into a coherent whole.

Danni seemed to have been thinking the same thing, because right then she whispered: "Yeah, that's it. Electra's nails are those of an impossibly aged crone—they're the only part of her body that the cannibal rejuvenation process doesn't affect."

"Huh?" Heather said, before realizing that Danni had merely been thinking aloud. Then she realized that Danni's outburst had answered her own question.

Pet was sitting on the floor beside Katie, leaning his head on her thigh. Katie began stroking his head. Staring at the captive girls, Pet soon got a fat erection and began licking Katie's leg, making her giggle. "Oh, stop that, you naughty doggie—you'll soon get me horny!"

Electra laughed and slipped a hand down the waistband of her shorts and began fingering herself.

Six-Six had been feeding some wood into the cooking fire. Now he strode over and stood beside Electra, once more holding his shotgun. Because of his giant size, Six-Six seemed the least affected by his alcohol consumption.

Runt had been standing in front of the girls all this while, swaying slightly on his feet and not saying anything. Him just standing there was enough to intimidate Heather, because in addition to Runt being naked except for his briefs, which gave her a full view of his broad and muscular and hairy body, the crotch of his briefs bulged like a tent. And Heather knew that her second-worst fears (the first were clearly her fears of being eaten) were about coming true.

Now, Runt gripped Danni's head and bent it first to the left and then to the right, then let go of it and did the same to Heather's head too. It seemed to Heather that he was trying to make up his mind which of them to rape first. And it didn't matter how tough a woman was, she would naturally feel horrified and apprehensive if she was going to be sexually assaulted and was powerless to stop it happening.

"I'm sure you two fine ladies are worrying over which of you I'm gonna fuck first," Runt said finally after letting go of Heather's head.

They stared at him, each dreading she'd be the one he'd pick, and then both gaped when he finally slid his underpants down his thighs and freed his erection. "No need to be scared you'll be left out, girls. Old Runt's gots enough dick for both of ya."

For the latest time tonight, Heather wished for the ground to open up and swallow her. Because Runt didn't have a normal penis. His erection was Y-shaped—yes, one shaft with two heads.

I am not frigging seeing this! Heather thought in disgust. She was unable to take her gaze from Runt's deformed member.

"Your penis is bifurcated!" Danni gasped.

Runt looked confused. "It's what?"

"Don't worry, bro. She's a silly know-it-all," Katie said. "Reads too many stupid books."

He's going to want us to suck him off, Heather thought in horror. *I just know it. He's gonna want us to suck on that horrible thing!* The thought of having to tend to Runt's penis with her lips and tongue was almost worse than her fear of death. Runt's manhood was just oh so gross. The entire penis was about six inches long overall, with the split happening three inches along the shaft, so that each of its ends was three inches long. Neither head was circumcised, and from the look of things, Runt hadn't washed his crotch in a long time. In addition to the smell coming from there, both penis heads had lots of smegma smeared over them from beneath their now retracted foreskins.

Heather looked over at Electra and Katie. Electra was fingering herself and moaning. Katie wasn't touching herself, but her eyes betrayed an intense lust. Pet was furiously humping Katie's leg with his erection, while Katie kept caressing his bald head.

Six-Six was rubbing his shotgun against his bulge, which now looked larger than before. Heather wondered if he had a two-headed penis too.

Runt said, "Now what I enjoy most of all while fucking a woman, is to double-penetrate her—fill both her holes at once. But see, tonight, I'm jest a li'l bit drunk, so all I'm gonna have you girls do is suck me off. I'll start double-fuckin' both of both your holes tomorrow."

"No!" Danni gasped. "Oh no, please!"

Runt frowned at her. "One more peep outa ya and I'll punch you so hard in the mouth that you'll swallow your damn braces. Alright?"

Danni nodded tearfully. Runt glared at Heather. She nodded back too.

"That's good. I love women who love to comply. Hey, Six-Six, give the shotgun to Katie and help me unhang these two bitches."

The giant handed his shotgun to Katie and walked over. A few seconds later Danni and Heather were down on their knees on the cave floor, with Runt's penis staring them both in the face.

"Oh shit!" Heather said as the muscular dwarf stepped forward and grabbed both she and Danni's heads and steered them towards his member. This was actually the only way it could possibly have worked anyway, because Heather's arms were so numb from being strung up overhead that they couldn't even support her weight when she tried to lean on them on the floor. So in that sense, Runt's steering her lips towards his penis's 'right-hand' head was a huge relief to her. She looked sideways at Danni. Danni was scowling with disgust and looked like she'd vomit. Heather felt the same. The dwarf reeked of wine and sweat and blood and the human flesh he'd just consumed. And the smegma too. His scrotum smelled like an entire NFL team before they hit the showers after a match.

Heather opened her mouth. The sooner Runt came, the sooner this horrible ordeal would be over with.

"Hey, bro, how 'bout if I fuck 'em both up the ass while they suck you off?" Six-Six asked brightly just as Runt's penis touched Heather's lips.

This caused a delay in proceedings, with the entire family laughing outrageously. "Hahahahahaha!"

"I'm serious!" Six-Six protested, pulling off his jockstrap. "I wanna fuck 'em too!"

Heather and Danni now both got a good look at Six-Six's erect penis. Both recoiled in horror. No, Six-Six didn't have a bifurcated penis; his own organ looked much worse. Heather had never imagined that a penis could look like this. It was both longer and thicker than her forearm, with the head as big as her fist; and was covered with immense bulges. Also, parts of it seemed plaited, as if the veins carrying its blood supply had gotten confused along the way and become knotted together. And then other parts of it looked scaly, as if covered with fish scales.

"If he touches me with that thing I'm gonna die instantly," Danni said, in a trembling voice that showed her to be close to fainting already.

Heather nodded silently. She was still staring at Six-Six's monstrous member. His testicles seemed to have mildew growing on them, and there seemed to be a line of additional fungi running along the penis's top also. *Oh, my dear God, that thing mustn't, totally mustn't, come anywhere near me!* Heather quailed.

Runt meanwhile, was laughing his head off. Six-Six stood there, his hands on his hips and his repellant penis throbbing threateningly. His eyes were wide with an innocent stupidity, as if he couldn't conceive of their actions being wrong.

Then Electra got to her feet. Swaying a little unsteadily, she smiled at her giant son.

"No, no no," she told Six-Six. "Come to momma, baby. You know you're too big for the silly little girls, you'll rip them to bits and kill them both. You can have them later, when we're ready to kill them— that way their flesh will remain fresh."

Six-Six stared over at his 'teenaged' mother, his eyes widening in delight when she stepped out of her shorts and bent over and shook her buttocks at him. "Come on now, honey," she cooed. "You know only momma can handle you like you like to be handled. Momma's the only real woman for you, you know that." Bent over holding her ankles like that, she looked ludicrously obscene, a porno parody of a high school's cutest cheerleader trying to seduce its largest and most moronic football player.

"Oh yeah!" Six-Six instantly seemed to forget about Heather and Danni. He headed for Electra, who straightened up and giggled when her giant son picked her up.

She shook her head at him when he tried to lay her down on the dinner table. "No, not out here, you naughty little boy," she said, then blew a kiss at him. "Let's go into the bedroom and do it on the nice soft bed where momma can spread her pussy really wide and accommodate all of you like you love it. You know what I mean, dear?"

"Hell yeah!" He picked her up again and slung her over his shoulder.

Heather was relieved when Six-Six carried Electra off into the room beyond the middle doorway, from which soon issued loud moaning noises.

Then Runt grabbed she and Danni by their ears and returned their faces to his penis. "Alright, girls, now that that touching family drama's been resolved, you two had best get back to sucking my cock. In fact, lets make a competition of it—let's see who comes first, me or Six-Six!" He gestured to Katie. "Hey, you be our timekeeper."

Katie shook her head. "Let's make it a real competition. Let's see who in the family can come first."

"Okay, let's," Runt agreed, holding Heather and Danni's mouths an inch away from his penis.

Katie pushed Pet away from humping her leg, then stood her shotgun upright against the chair that Electra had recently vacated. That done, she pulled down her shorts and kicked them away. Pet growled impatiently at her.

"Wait, kid," was all she told the deformed teen, patting him on the head while doing so. Then she turned back to the table and seemed to fiddle around with the dinner remains for a while. Heather and Danni heard a loud snapping noise, but didn't know what had made it.

When Katie turned around again, she held a half-empty wine bottle in her left hand. Her right hand gripped the humerus—the upper arm bone—of the human arm that Six-Six had had for dinner.

While Runt chuckled, Katie suggestively licked the bone's smooth ball-joint.

"That damn thing's almost as big as Six-Six's cock," Runt joked.

"Hell, don't I know it?" Katie replied with a lewd wink.

That said, she placed the rounded head of the bone down between her legs. "Alright, on my *cunt* of three. That okay with you?"

Runt nodded, both of his penis heads poised a half-inch from the captive girls' quivering lips. "Yeah. Hey—what's the prize for whoever wins?"

A torrent of loud moans spilled out of the bedroom, making Katie laugh. "I think Electra already won."

She took a drink of wine from the bottle, then snapped her fingers at Pet, who'd been sitting obediently by the chair, trying to fellate himself, but not succeeding because his mouth couldn't reach an additional two inches down to suck on the head of his swollen penis. Pet looked up at Katie, nodding expectantly, and with his tongue dangling from his lips like he was really a dog.

"Hey, boy, you can resume humping now. You're in the competition too, okay?"

Pet nodded eagerly (which was Heather's first clue that the kid wasn't completely stupid), then he bounded over to Katie's outstretched left leg and began rubbing his erection against it again.

As far as Heather could tell, Pet was about one third as intelligent as Six-Six, which was maybe just as intelligent as a real dog—he understood 'fetch' and 'sit' commands, and such like, but lacked any real power to think for himself.

Runt said, "How 'bout if . . . whoever wins decides how we kill these two girls? And which one dies first."

"Hey, that's a really cool prize," Katie drunkenly agreed, then she pointed down at Pet. "He seems about to come though. What if Pet wins?"

"We'll let him fuck 'em both first. Then *we'll* flip a coin and decide."

Katie nodded. "Ha ha ha! Alright, start on my signal, and you two sluts, no cheating, okay? All you do is suck on his cock—one dickhead per girl and no switchovers. No fingering his balls or licking his asshole or sticking a finger up it to press on his prostate . . . if you do I'll cut your ears off." After a final swig of wine, Katie held the humerus bone tightly with both hands and said: "Alright, on my *cunt* of three: one . . . two . . . three!"

Heather gasped as Katie sank the head of the human arm bone deep into her vagina. Katie gasped in what sounded like pain, then began masturbating with the bone.

"Holy shit!" Danni gasped too. "She's crazy, she's—!"

But that was when Runt forced both of their mouths down on his penis. "Start suckin', you bitches. Don't you dare let me lose this competition." He bent down and grabbed a hold of one of each of their breasts and tweaked them painfully. "An' lemme warn ya—whichever one of you puts in the least effort's gonna die first—remember I can feel what each of you's doin' down there!"

Heather needed no further encouragement. She began sucking fiercely on Runt's dirty member. Her face was right next to Danni's so she could see the horror and disgust in Danni's eyes as she too fellated their tormentor.

"Yeah," Runt groaned. "Two girls, one cock? I should be in porn, I tell ya!"

"I'm gonna win ya yet, dwarf!" Katie gasped. They couldn't see her or Pet either—Danni had her back turned to Katie and was also in Heather's way—but they could hear her loud and clear. She was moaning loudly with pleasure now and Pet was barking and growling too.

Heather concentrated on Katie's moans of sexual delight—her shift of mental focus helped her perform this demeaning act of fellatio. She shut her eyes and sucked, imagining that she, and not Katie, was the one gasping out her enjoyment, imagining away the rancid smegma taste and stale sweaty smell and her fear that this sexual contact between Runt and herself was certain to result in her catching some incurable social disease.

I'll worry about that after I survive this.

Runt was running his hands through her hair and his gasps were almost as loud as Katie's. "Oh shit, gal, you're so good at sucking cock, I might keep you alive for a month as least."

Heather hoped she was the one he was referring to and not Danni. And then a sudden horrified suspicion filled her and she opened her eyes again. She discovered it was just as she'd suspected: Danni had stopped sucking on her end of Runt's penis. She had an enraged look in her eyes and was . . . well, her mouth was open wide and her cheek muscles were bunched up tight and the muscles in her neck were standing out like cords and her teeth were gleaming white and dangerous behind their silver braces and . . .

Hell no! Heather thought desperately. She shoved Danni away at the same moment that Danni brought her teeth together. Then, not bothering to look at her companion, or at Katie for that matter (who was now moaning loud endearments to someone called 'Boku Voss'), she slipped her mouth off the end of Runt's bifurcated penis, grabbed one of its heads in each hand and began vigorously masturbating the dwarf. With her wrists still bound, she could just manage this manual stimulation.

It helped that Runt was about coming anyway. Suddenly he howled, "Oh, fucking fuckity fuck!" and ejaculated all over Heather's face. The come squirted from both tips of his penis at once, initially hitting Heather in both eyes. Blinded for the moment, she kept on masturbating Runt, then slipped her mouth down over each penis head in turn and began sucking it off. She kept this up until Runt's erection began deflating.

"Shiiiit!" Runt gasped finally, pushing Heather's head away from his manhood. "Oh, my fucking God!"

He stared down at Danni, who was lying sprawled on the floor after Heather had shoved her away from him (though he'd not realized that she'd been about biting his penis off). Before he could comment though, he realized that Katie was still masturbating. Katie had her eyes closed and the arm bone sunk more than halfway into her vagina, where she was twisting and turning it with a firm two-handed grip. She was gasping as if she was about coming herself. Pet was still humping away furiously at her left leg.

"Hey . . . I won the contest!" Runt yelled happily. "I won, I won!" He danced over to his sister's side and tapped her on the shoulder. "I won, bitch! I frigging won!"

Katie opened her eyes as slits. "Okay, yeah, you won. Now shut up, dwarf, I'm about coming here!"

"Shit, I've told you all—I ain't a goddamn dwarf!" But he turned away from her as she shut her eyes again and instead reached for the wine bottle. Standing there with a smile on his face, he tilted the bottle up until it was vertical and glugged down almost all the wine left in it.

Heather, who'd now wiped Runt's come out of her eyes, took this interlude to pull Danni up. With no further need for them to kneel down, both young women got back to their feet.

"Don't you ever dare try and pull another stupid stunt like that," Heather whispered angrily to her friend. "What the hell were you thinking? Are you trying to get us both killed?"

"I'm sorry," Danni whispered back tearily. "I just couldn't help myself. His smell and stink and everything about him is just so nauseating and . . . it just entered my head then to bite his cock off and that we'd both be okay if I did so."

Heather, the taste of Runt's semen still fresh on her tongue, easily sympathized. "Just try to control yourself," she cautioned. "These guys aren't playing nice."

Danni nodded. "We just need to wait for them to go to sleep and then we can discuss our options for getting away."

Heather wanted to hug her, but with both their wrists bound this was impossible. So instead she said, "Good girl, that's what I want to hear. You're right, it has to be close to midnight now. Soon they'll all—"

"Oh fuck, I'm coming!" Katie moaned.

Heather and Danni turned and gaped at her. Katie was stirring the humerus bone around in her vagina like her body was a stewpot. "Oh God, oh my fucking God . . . oh oh oh oh oh . . . !"

She went limp, letting her arms fall to her sides and leaving the bone sticking from her crotch like an erect penis. Pet immediately left off humping Katie's leg and grabbed the bone between his teeth, trying to pull it out of her vagina. His efforts merely resulted in Katie moaning in pleasure again. After watching for a while, Runt took pity on Pet and pulled the bone out of Katie and dropped it on the floor between her legs. Pet instantly leapt on it and began licking Katie's sexual lubrication off of it. Katie lifted her legs off the floor and placed them on Pet's back while he licked the bone. She began rubbing her clitoris and trying for a second orgasm.

"This is so goddamn perverse that I think I'm dreaming it," Heather said.

"I wish I *was* dreaming," Danni said. "Then I could wake up and this nightmare would have ended."

"This will soon be over," Heather said comfortingly. "And they'll fall asleep like their slut mom and retarded brother and then we can plan."

But no, their ordeal *wasn't* over yet.

Swaying a little drunkenly as he stood by the dinner table, and with his penis swaying like an upside-down 'Y,' Runt said, "Hey, Pet still ain't come."

Katie shrugged. "Same reason as usual—his fingers ain't long enough to grip his dick properly, so he can't jerk off right. He just gets all frustrated rubbin' against me, but if I stop him he gets upset instead."

"You gonna jerk him off then, seeing as you're the one who's got him so excited?"

Katie shook her head. "Hell no, that's too gross to even consider."

Runt laughed. "C'mon, Katie, give the dog's bone a break."

Katie shook her head vigorously. "Hey, I may be drunk, dwarf, but I ain't *that* drunk. I got principles, okay?—and there's some things that I just ain't doin', no matter how much wine I got in me. Let Electra wank him off; she don't mind who she fucks."

"She's asleep. Listen, I'm not sure whose snores are louder, our 'kid' mama or our kid brother."

"So Pet's just gonna have to wait till morning then."

"No need for him to go without tonight," Runt said, settling himself down in a chair and picking up the shotgun and stroking it. "I got a much better idea: let one of your sexy friends suck him off. Or better still, both of 'em at once, like they did me."

"Hey, that's a great idea! Hey, Pet, c'mere boy!"

The dog-teen bounded over.

Katie pointed over at Heather and Danni. "Alright, boy, pick one of those two to be your bitch tonight. You're gonna come too, okay? You're gonna shoot a hot load up those girls."

Pet began leaping up and down excitedly.

"Aw shit," Danni groaned. "Doesn't this crap ever end? First the dwarf and now their dog mutant?"

"Shush, they'll hear you."

Danni shook her head. "We're in no danger there. They're both too drunk to pay much attention. That bitch Katie can hardly stand up. And how big a pussy must you have in order to shove an entire arm bone up it and not kill yourself?"

"Shush!" Heather repeated. "Here he comes!"

Pet had reached them now. First of all, he sniffed Danni's ass, then bounded around her and tried to sniff her crotch. Danni stood there like she was paralyzed, with her hands in front of her, so Pet couldn't get his nose up between her legs.

"Hey, let the doggie make his choice," Katie called out. "Or else . . ."

But Pet had already lost interest in Danni. Now he moved over to Heather and began sniffing her instead.

At first Heather endured the humiliation of having the deformed teenager sniffing between her buttocks and licking her there till she felt like she might shit. Pet, however, seemed to like her, or at least to prefer her to Danni. Heather found this completely unacceptable.

Why me? This is just so damned unfair!

And then after nosing between her buttocks, Pet moved around and began licking her vagina. His tongue was very rough and it hurt her soft vaginal lips.

"Hey, I think the doggie likes her," Runt called out.

"Yeah," Katie drunkenly agreed. She'd produced another bottle of red wine now and was sloshing it down, not caring that a fair amount of the liquor was going to waste because it was spilling down onto her breasts. "Wow, look at how hard Pet's dick is!"

"And it's drippin' too! It's really drippin' with pre-come. Alright, git 'er, boy. Give the bitch some doggie lovin'!"

Katie nodded. "Alright, Heather, you know the fucking deal here. Doggy-style, get down on your hands and knees, and spread your ass wide for the kid!"

It was then that it happened. Heather didn't know what came over her then. Maybe it was the sight and feel of Pet's stunted 'fingers' pawing her thighs and breasts, while his tongue lolled from the left side of his mouth and dripped saliva between his horrid malformed teeth; maybe it was Katie's mocking laugh and Runt's jeering (he was getting sexually excited again while watching this: his penis was stiff and he was masturbating with a hand on each of its twin heads); or maybe it was simply the fact that she was about to be subjected to further humiliation while Danni would be let off; maybe it was even just that the heat from the fire under the stewpot felt like it was baking her skin . . . but something snapped in Heather's head right then, and instead of getting down on her hands and knees like Katie was ordering, she lashed out instead.

It was a subconscious revolt, of course. She acted entirely without thinking, her feeling of overwhelming revulsion for her humiliating situation suddenly inverting and converting into violent anger.

The upshot of this was that right as Pet was leaping up from the floor to clamp his misshapen teeth on her right nipple, Heather lashed out with her right knee.

The effect was immediate and brutal. Her knee met Pet's jaw. Pet fell back to the floor whimpering in pain. He wasn't out cold, but wasn't far from it either, the blow having completely stunned him. He was also bleeding from the mouth.

Heather had a moment of relief at apparently being spared this second rape of the night, and then Katie was up off her chair and raging furiously at her.

Katie charged at Heather, flinging the wine bottle at her as she came. Heather just managed to get out of the way. The bottle whirled through the air, spilling its red contents and creating the effect of a Catherine wheel firework, before shattering against the stacked cords of wood by the far wall.

By then, however, Katie had a firm grip on Heather's hair, and was yanking her head painfully to the side.

"ARE YOU GODAMMN CRAZY!" she screamed in Heather's face.

Heather looked behind Katie, at Pet, who was still lying on the ground with his eyes crossed. True, there was quite a lot of blood by the kid's head, but she didn't see what Katie was so mad about.

"I'm gonna frigging *hurt* you for doing that to Pet!" Katie said, with a deadly facial expression now replacing her initial rage. "You almost killed him!"

"Dammit," Runt said, kneeling beside Pet and rolling him on his back, "It sure don't look like Pet's gettin' laid tonight after all."

Katie really looked insane enough to kill Heather.

"I didn't mean to!" Heather blurted out. "Besides, he's just a dog, right? He's just your doggie! Katie, calm down, I'll suck him off tomorrow, I promise I will!" While speaking, Heather glanced sideways at Danni. Danni looked confused.

"Just my doggie?" Katie let go of Heather's hair and took a step backward. "Just a doggie? We just call him that. He's my *son*, you stupid bitch! My *son*, and you just tried to kill him." She turned and stared worriedly at Pet, then at her brother. "Is he okay?"

Runt nodded. "He's alright. His dick's gone down now though."

Katie turned back towards Heather. "Alright, I've had just about enough of both of you dumb bitches. Now I'm gonna teach you a lesson."

"Look, I said I'm sorry! I promise it won't happen again!" Heather couldn't get her mind around the fact that Pet—that deformed, subnormal cretin—was Katie's son. *Her damn son? How old is she really then? He looks to be about fourteen, and she told us that she's twenty one. So at what age did she have him? When she was seven years old?*

"Honest, it won't happen again, Katie," Danni pleaded too.

Katie laughed coldly. "Oh, it definitely won't happen again. When I'm done with her, she'll know better than to mess with my kids."

Oh Christ, Heather thought. *I'm dead for sure now.*

Heather's eyes instantly went to the oaken worktable beside the ever-bubbling stewpot, with its array of knives and cleavers. Adding to her terror was the sight of the heaped mass of Maude's remains which still sat in their basin by the fire, waiting to be added to the cooking meat, a task that Electra had seemingly forgotten about before going off to be sexed to sleep by her giant son.

"Hey, Pet, fetch mommy a knife," Katie said brightly.

Pet was wheezing and still looked stunned, but he was back on his feet again. He stared at Heather with a mixture of dread and anger; baring his teeth at her and growling in a low rumble. Most of the blood on him was from a tear in his upper lip where her knee had connected with it.

"Knife for mommy, honey, so mommy can punish the wicked girls," Katie told Pet.

Pet scampered off to the worktable. He leaned up on his paw-like hands, nosing left and right across the arrayed knives, with his eyes darting to and fro as if he was trying to make up his mind, and then finally settled on a short knife with a thin blade. Because his fingers were too stump-like to pick up the knife, he pulled it towards his mouth and got a good hold on the grip with his teeth. Then he trotted back to Katie's side and wagged his head at her.

"Good doggie." Katie took the knife from her son's mouth and patted him fondly on the head.

Katie waved the knife at Heather.

"Don't hurt me," Heather gasped. "Please don't."

Heather laughed. "Oh, but I am gonna hurt you like you hurt him. Hell, girl, I'm gonna hurt you even more than you hurt Pet."

Pet began leaping and down in excitement.

"What'cha gonna do to her?" Runt asked Katie as she glared at Heather, who simply couldn't meet her eyes. He'd picked up his shotgun again, clearly to forestall any attempts at flight or resistance.

Katie laughed. "I'm gonna disfigure the bitch, that's what. She thinks she's too good for my son 'cos she's really pretty. So I'm gonna take her pride down a few notches, make her a freak too." She grabbed hold of Heather's chin and tilted her face up. "Bitch, I'm gonna slice off both of your cute ears and your stuck-up nose, and then I'm gonna roast them on a skewer so Pet can have them for his breakfast."

"No!" Heather howled in horror. "No!"

She turned to run, but Katie quickly grabbed hold of her again. Then Katie kneed her in the groin. Heather folded forward. Next, Katie clubbed her over the head so she collapsed to the floor. She lay there stunned, exactly like Pet had a short while ago. Next thing she knew, Katie was kneeling over her with a crazy glint in her eyes and the knife was coming close to her face.

"No!" Heather moaned gently. "Don't!" She was completely helpless. In addition to the fact that she was so stunned that she felt completely discombobulated, Katie was sitting on her belly, pinning her bound hands in place at her crotch.

"Say 'bye to your nose, pretty bitch!" Katie said, digging her fingers up Heather's nostrils and placing the knife against the side of her nose.

"No!" Heather moaned again in a weak voice that sounded like fading hopes. "Help, somebody!"

Help came from a completely unexpected source.

"Hey, wait!" Runt called, walking over.

The knife pressed into Heather's nose, but didn't cut just yet.

"What is it?" Katie asked impatiently.

Shotgun slung over his shoulder, the dwarf stood beside them cleaning his left nostril with a pinky finger. "Well, see, I figure the girl deserves a reward 'cos she helped me win our li'l sex competition."

Katie fumed. "That has nothing to do with this!"

Heather prayed that it did.

"I like her," Runt said after flicking a ball of snot away in Danni's direction. (Danni didn't move as the snot struck her left breast and stuck there. She had been watching, terrified. She was so relieved that she wasn't the one to be mutilated. She was intent on becoming a statue; she wanted the cannibals to forget she existed.)

"I really like her," Runt repeated, pointing down at Heather. "She sucks dick like a champ; ain't never had a girl jerk me off with both hands that well." He grinned down at Heather. "Well, my point is that suckin' a guy's cock that good deserves a reward, and since I won, I can't let you cut her ears and nose off. I want her to suck me off again and I don't want her deformed while doin' so."

Katie scowled at him. But she took the knife away from Heather's nose, which made Heather breathe out in deep relief. "Oh, alright, but I promised Pet some of her flesh. How 'bout if I cut off just *one* of her ears. She's got long hair, you won't notice that while she's suckin' you off. Besides, it'll provide her with great motivation to do a better job next time or lose the other ear."

Runt shook his head. "Nah, I got a better idea." He turned and pointed to Danni. "Cut *her* ears and nose off. That way Pet'll still have his two ears and a nose for breakfast, and you'll still get to take out your rage on someone. And I'll still get some grade-A cocksuckin' until we decide to cook both of 'em." He flicked his penis a few times, then gestured dismissively at Danni: "This one's useless at suckin' dick—I could feel the left head gettin' soft while she was workin' on it."

"No no no!" Danni gasped in horror as all four sets of eyes now turned on her. "It's not my fault!"

"Hell yeah, that's a great idea," Katie agreed with a broad grin as she got up off Heather.

Heather shared Danni's fright. She felt that she should plead for Danni, but she didn't. She couldn't. She hoped that this was all a practical joke, that the cannibal siblings would spare Danni at the last moment and go to bed instead.

"Okay, so you got your cocksucker," Katie said, throwing an amused look back at Heather. "Hey, bitch, you're still pretty. Just make sure you swallow next time, huh, or I'll sever your tits?"

Heather nodded quickly and vigorously. Katie turned back to Danni. "Well, girl, you're gonna provide my son Pet with a li'l sweet flesh!"

"You can't do this to me!" Danni protested. "I didn't do anything. I didn't kick your son. It wasn't me!"

Danni turned and ran, but she went the wrong way, and tripped over Pet, who'd been hurrying toward her. Yelping, Pet scrambled out of her way, but Danni went down flat on her face anyway.

After that it was all academic. Katie rolled Danni over onto her back and sat on her belly. With both of them so positioned, Heather was spared the sight of what transpired, but hearing Danni's relentless screaming and seeing the ceaseless kicking of her feet as Katie worked on her was enough to terrify her afresh.

Runt stood aside watching with his Y-shaped penis erect again.

Then there was a weird interlude when a naked Electra Hemingway suddenly appeared in the open middle doorway:

"Hey, you damn kids, stop making that damn racket, I'm trying to sleep in here," she said drowsily, somehow making herself audible over Danni's screams. Then she immediately retreated again and shut the bedroom door behind her.

Katie and Runt began laughing. "Mom's really drunk tonight," Runt said. Then he came over and pushed Heather down to her knees again, and shoved his hard penis into her mouth.

"Yeah," he said as Heather got to work on him with both hands. "That's a beautiful cocksucker."

Danni's screams of pain had really turned him on. This time it took less than a minute for Runt to come. And this time Heather made sure that she swallowed as much of his semen as she could, switching rapidly from penis-head to penis-head as each squirted its disgusting liquid load at her face, and trying to pinch each urethra shut when her mouth wasn't on it, and then finally pushing both of Runt's ejaculating glanses together and forcing her lips around them so that her cheeks bulged out like a chipmunk's. It wasn't just Katie's threat motivating her—the fellatio was also something to take her mind off of what was occurring just a few yards away.

By the time that Runt had finished ejaculating, Katie too was finished with Danni.

Heather looked over at her friend, who lay sobbing hysterically on the ground. Danni no longer had a nose—there was just a frothy bloody hole in the middle of her face—and both sides of her head were covered with blood too. In fact most of Danni's head and shoulders was covered with blood.

For her part, Katie seemed very pleased with herself. With Pet barking happily along beside her in anticipation of his breakfast, Katie made her way to the kitchen table and got a thin skewer. Then she speared Danni's ears and nose on the skewer and set the skewer in the kebab stand beside Maude's roasting kidneys and heart and tongue.

"Hey, Runt, I think these kidneys are done!" she called. "You know how Electra gets if the meat's overcooked."

"Yeah, and it's 'bout time I added your other friend's meat to the pot anyway. Shit, I sure wish you'd remembered to bring those spices along."

"Hey, midget, don't you dare fucking start on me 'bout that again. I'm so not in the mood for your bullshit tonight!"

"Fuck you, Katie, I'm not a goddamn midget!" A scowl on his ugly face, Runt walked over to join Katie by the fire.

Once he wasn't watching her, Heather scurried over to Danni's side.

Oh my God! How could they do this to her? The sight of her mutilated friend terrified her.

"Oh, I'm so so sorry I did this to you," she told Danni. "This is all my stupid fault."

Then: "Yeow!" she screamed as a sharp pain bit her in her right ankle.

She spun around to see that Pet had her by the ankle—his jaws locked around it—and was shaking it and biting down hard enough to make her ankle bleed.

This time it was very easy for Heather to resist kicking Pet. She had no desire to end up like Danni, earless and noseless and covered in blood like it was makeup. At the moment Danni looked like a circus freak. Heather also suspected that maybe Pet—who clearly wasn't completely dumb—might be doing this intentionally, trying to instigate her into kicking him again, so that . . . maybe the deformed bastard wanted more ears and her own nose for breakfast too.

"Let go of me!" she screamed at Pet, but made no attempt to touch him or kick him away.

"He don't like you," Runt called. "You'd better keep that in mind 'cos he'll be the one watchdogging you girls while everyone else is asleep."

"Yeah," Katie added. "And here's the thing: Pet's got the most sensitive ears imaginable, and he don't sleep at all anytime we've got captives. So if you dare try to escape from the cage we'll know and then we'll *really* do a number on you two bitches."

"Yes, yes!" Heather agreed with tears dribbling down her cheeks as Pet continued to relentlessly chew on her ankle, "but I think he's biting my foot off."

"If he doesn't stop she's gonna bleed to death," Danni said suddenly, in an eerily calm though trembling voice. "Take my word for it."

"Oh, okay, nerd," Katie reluctantly agreed. "Alright, Pet, that's enough fun for tonight. Hey, doggie, mommy said that's enough! Let go of her damn leg right now or it's no breakfast for you!"

Heather was relieved when the canine youth removed his jaws from her ankle and backed away from her, though not without first licking her crotch and getting another erection. So maybe it wasn't that Pet disliked her, but that he wanted her and was pissed off that he wasn't getting her tonight. Sexual frustration did that to people; even to complete retards apparently.

Once he'd left her alone, she examined her ankle. Pet's teeth had left deep pits in her flesh and there was some red seeping, but actually his teeth had hardly broken through her skin, and what bleeding there was was manageable. *But . . . shit, it felt like he was really breaking my ankle. I hope I can still walk.*

She flexed her bound wrists as much as she could, wishing someone would untie them. Her fingers had begun feeling numb again.

"Alright, girls," Runt said, leaving Katie's side by the worktable, "let's get you both locked up in the cage for the night."

This was a relief to hear. Heather helped Danni to her feet, and then, limping along—it was impossible to place any weight on her right foot—she let Runt herd them towards the cage and lock them inside it.

Now she understood how all the bloodstains had gotten on it.

"I'm sorry, Danni," she said after Runt had returned to join Katie by the cannibal's cooking fire. "I'm really, really, really sorry that I made them do this to you."

But Danni didn't reply. Instead she smiled at Heather. And there was something terrifying in that smile that Danni gave Heather—bloodied and still bleeding and noseless, earless Danni who had to be in incredible agony, both of body and mind—something intensely horrific in her smile that made Heather lose it.

Because, Heather fainted then. She didn't intend to, but emptiness suddenly filled her mind and her soul and overcame her, as if a wind of terror had blown through her head and flushed the night's awful happenings away.

So Heather passed out, with the last image in her mind as unconsciousness overtook her being the image of her mutilated friend's blood-drenched face, with that expression of the 'Angel of Death' plastered all over it.

CHAPTER 17

I See Me

After escaping from his captor Hank Rollins, Jory Haines had at first tried to find the highway.

Unfortunately though, in his blind panic while fleeing Hank, he'd headed the wrong way through the forest at the foot of Misery Mountain and had gotten lost. Even with the aid of the flashlight, all the trees looked the same types.

Then Jory had calmed down enough to realize two important things. First, that by now Hank would very likely be pursuing him; and second, that the flashlight beam would give him away. So he'd switched off his flashlight and tried to navigate the forest by the light of the moon.

It was now that Jory accidentally went the *right* way and wound up at the clearing where Hank's black Jeep Cherokee was parked.

At first he'd been delighted. He simply had to steal the vehicle and drive off in it. But then he'd remembered that Hank had the Jeep's keys on him; which meant that stealing the Jeep was out of the question.

It was right then that Jory had caught sight of Hank's own flashlight coming towards him through the trees.

Scared, but relieved that he'd not yet entered the clearing himself, Jory had hidden behind a pine trunk and watched Hank approach the Jeep, sit on it, and then open it up and fiddle around inside it. He'd considered rushing at Hank and trying to overpower him, but truth be told, Jory wasn't much of a fighter and had quickly decided that discretion was the better part of valor.

So he'd just watched Hank and waited quietly till Hank had stalked off into the woods again.

So what to do now?

Jory had then realized that he had no way of finding his way out of the forest tonight. Not with Hank hunting him. He'd thought for a long while and finally decided that his best chance was to climb a tree and hide till morning.

And if I climb one near this clearing, I can keep a good watch on this madman who abducted me in the first place.

So that's what Jory did. After waiting a while longer to make certain that Hank wouldn't return to the clearing, he'd looked around for a suitable tree, a large one with branches low enough for him to climb up onto.

And that's where he was now. Sitting up in an oak tree, at the joint of his chosen branch and the main trunk, about ten feet above the forest floor.

His vantage position had already paid off. Twice now, Hank had walked right beneath him. The second time Hank had been angrily muttering, "When I catch that young punk, I'm gonna feed him this shotgun barrel for breakfast!"

That statement convinced Jory of the wisdom of his keeping quieter than a mouse.

Hank had since left the clearing again. He'd been gone for about twenty minutes now. Jory didn't know if Hank was intentionally returning to the clearing, or if he was getting lost himself and finding himself back here by mistake.

Whichever was the case, Jory figured he was safe up here till morning.

After making certain that he was securely perched on his branch and wouldn't accidentally roll out of the tree, he shut his eyes and went to sleep.

He awoke suddenly and swiftly. Jory had no idea how long he'd slept for, but he had the intuitive knowledge that he wasn't alone in the tree. Something had touched him and that touch had woken him up.

He froze against the oak and listened carefully, trying to hear if maybe Hank was beneath him and had thrown up a rock to check if there was anyone up there amidst the tree's leaves.

But he heard no sounds below him. The night was alive with sounds, but they were the normal nocturnal forest sounds of small animals going about their business.

A sudden fear now gripped Jory. He felt certain that he wasn't alone in this oak tree. He had the chilling impression that something was watching him from the cluster of leaves on his left, where one of the oak's higher branches dipped down and smothered another branch at his own level. The nearer part of that branch was less than a yard from Jory, a short enough distance for someone to stretch across an arm and touch him.

Okay, I'm losing it here, he thought. *That was most likely just a squirrel . . . or a chipmunk. I need to calm down. It'll be completely stupid of me, the most dumb thing ever, to scare myself so much that I give my position away to Hank.*

But Jory couldn't convince himself that he was alone in the oak tree. Now he could practically feel that unseen pair of eyes examining his body. And he also sensed something else as well—a raging hunger directed at him—though how he could sense this latter, he didn't know.

Finally, when his dread had him near to jumping out of the tree and damning the consequences, Jory flicked the flashlight on for a quick look in the direction from which he kept sensing his unseen companion's presence.

At first Jory didn't understand what he was seeing. Yes, there was someone sitting on that nearby branch, his body slightly buried amidst the leaves and as such not presenting a clear outline. But . . . but . . . but . . .

That's me over there! How's that possible? Did someone hang a mirror up here? But why would anyone do that?

But Jory quickly realized that the version of himself on the other branch wasn't really his reflection. Because no one had a moving reflection, did they? And this one was coming towards him. Coming fast, in a clear hurry to get to him. And as it came, this doppelganger began altering, its clothes turning into warty brown skin with the same ease with which a chameleon switched colors.

Even before his 'reflection' had completed its transformation, Jory realized that he was looking at the monster which Hank wanted to trap.

So Hank wasn't lying after all? Oh shit, where the hell is he now?

All of a sudden Jory Haines wanted the man he was hiding from to be right beside him, protecting him.

"Hank!" he screamed as the monster leapt across the gap separating the branches and slammed into him. "Hank, it's over here! It's got me!"

He tried to shove the monster off of him, but before he could manage to do so he felt a horrible pain in his belly. He shined his flashlight down and saw that the creature—now a horrible long-limbed thing with a diamond-shaped head that had a single ruby-red eye—had both of its hands deep inside his belly. And he could feel its claws tearing him up inside, slicing through his body's tissues and the sinews and ligaments that held him together.

"HANK, HELP ME PLEEEEEASE!" Jory screamed in terror and agony as the monster tore all of his intestines out of his belly.

CHAPTER 18

The Plan

When Heather opened her eyes, she was surprised to find herself staring up at a Muslim girl wearing a hijab and a red veil. The girl was shaking her vigorously.

"Hey, wake up!" she was also loudly whispering.

It took a moment for Heather to realize that she was looking at Danni. Danni had wrapped a tee shirt around her head and neck, and her head seemed eerily distorted in the now-dim cave lighting. The tee shirt she'd used was white, and in the endless shadows cast by the flickering fire under the cooking pot, made her look like a serial killer. This effect was somewhat dulled though by the fact that the rest of Danni's body was naked.

Like rancid sewage pouring from an exploded sewage truck and flooding the highway, bad memories rushed into Heather's head. She remembered exactly where she was and why she was here, and also why Danni was covering her face like this.

She glanced quickly around the cave, but saw no one. Their captors had all apparently retired for the night. A twinge of pain in her right ankle reminded her also of how Pet had savaged it. She flexed the ankle. It was better now, just a little stiff.

She returned her attention to Danni. Danni's 'nosebleed' seemed to have stopped. She had a dark patch where her nose had been, and two other dark patches on either side of her head, but seemed otherwise okay.

Heather was more worried by the slightly crazed look in her friend's eyes. That and the fact that she seemed to be grinning broadly beneath her white mask.

"What's funny?" she asked with an intense shudder. Because, she knew that if she'd been the one thus mutilated, mirth of any sort would be the furthest thing from her mind.

But Danni just shrugged and waved a finger in the air. And that was when Heather realized that her friend's hands were now untied. She looked around for the rope Danni's wrists had been bound with. It lay in two bloody halves beside a sharp steel projection on the cage's mesh wall.

"I didn't feel up to using my teeth to untie the knots," Danni quickly explained, her voice slightly muffled by the fabric stretched across her mouth. "Alright, hold out your hands and let me untie you too."

"Oh yes, thanks." Heather stuck out her hands and waited while Danni fiddled with the knots. Soon her own wrists were free too. With relief she began massaging the circulation back into them. "What now?" she asked.

"Time we were leaving," Danni said, grinning her crazy grin again.

That got Heather's full attention. "Leaving? How? We're locked in."

Danni laughed and it was the creepiest sound that Heather had ever heard in her life. "Not for long, we aren't. In fact, here comes our rescuer right now."

Still confused, Heather turned and saw that Pet was silently padding over towards them, his deformed body jerking from side to side with his lopsided gait.

"Yeah, his mom was right," Danni said. "The little shithead apparently never sleeps. He's been prowling around the cave for hours."

"How long was I out for?"

"Maybe three hours. I haven't slept myself. I didn't want to wake you until I'd worked everything out."

Heather felt a surge of relief. *Alright, so maybe Danni is going a little round the bend with this smiling act of hers, but at least her wonderful brain still works.*

Pet had meanwhile reached them. Seeing that Heather was awake now, he snuggled against her side of the cage and began licking her right thigh, which was pressed against a gap in the cage wall.

"No," Danni cautioned, when Heather moved her hand to shove Pet away. Then she leaned close and whispered, "He wants you. He's been sniffing away at you ever since you dropped off. If your anus feels a little wet now, that's 'cos he's been licking it."

"And you let him?" Heather whispered back in disgust. Yes, she realized that her whole anal crack did feel wet and sticky. "How could you?" she asked, looking down at the deformed teenager who was still licking her thigh. She also realized that he wasn't making a sound.

"What happened to him?" she asked Danni. "Cat got the doggie's tongue?"

"I told him to be quiet if he wanted you."

Heather looked down at Pet again, and this time she easily recognized the look of lust in his eyes. She also saw that the dog-teen had an erection again. "Huh? Oh, no. Noooo."

Danni placed a hand over her mouth to shush her. "Look, don't ruin things for us. It's our only way out of here."

"I don't see a way out. We're locked in here and he's out there."

"Not for much longer. Just trust me and do exactly what I tell you to do, without any questions." She leaned away from Heather. "Think you can handle that?"

Heather felt insulted by the question, but staring at Danni, whose lips were once more parted against the tee shirt fabric in a smile, she nodded.

"There had better be a method to your madness," she said.

"Oh, there fucking is. Wait and see."

"What now?"

"Just get ready and follow my lead. Remember, do whatever I instruct you to."

Danni moved to the edge of the cage and signaled Pet over to her. Heather was amazed at how sure her actions were.

"Hey listen, doggie," she whispered, patting Pet on the head while he drooled against the cell bars. "Now, remember what I told you: You're gonna fuck her juicy ass really good, but first of all you need to get the keys so you can get into the cage with us and we can all have a really fun time, alright?"

She spoke in a low, seductive whisper. Pet nodded vigorously back, but silently. Danni had clearly cautioned him on the need for silence.

"Alright, doggie baby," Danni cooed. "Now look over there. See the keys on the table where Uncle Runt left them for you? You just go and fetch 'em now. But you gotta be quiet and not wake up either

Momma Katie or Grandma Electra or Uncle Six-Six or mean Uncle Runt either." She looked sternly at Pet. "Can you do that, honey?"

His nods of assent became even more assenting when she grabbed his stiff penis through the bars and gave it a firm jerk.

"Alright, doggie, now hurry up. And as a bonus, I'll suck you off first. How's that? And after this you're still gonna eat my ears for breakfast!"

Pet turned and loped off on all fours towards the dinner table.

"What now?" Heather asked once she thought he was out of earshot.

"He brings back the key, and we fuck him and kill him and escape. It's that simple. The cage has a padlock that's easy to reach. I've tried reaching it and I'm sure I can get the lock open."

Heather looked over at Pet, who was now sniffing up at the dining table, and shook her head in disgust. "Girl, you're mad. I am not having sex with that thing."

"I'll do it—I'll fuck him. You just keep him quiet and kill him."

"Kill him? How?"

"Strangle him, it's important that he doesn't make a sound while dying. All the doors are shut and everyone's fast asleep. If you listen you can hear Katie snoring though her bedroom door."

"Okay, but after that how do we leave this place?"

"Shush, here he comes with the key."

Heather turned. Pet was bounding towards them with the key in his mouth. He paused by the cage and looked shyly up at Danni.

"Good doggie," she said, stroking his bald head, then she turned to Heather and whispered, "Alright, you keep him happy while I get the lock open."

"How?"

"Jerk him off. But not too hard, we don't want him coming just yet."

Heather felt disgusted, but she did it. She slipped her hand between Pet's legs and grabbed his swollen member. It was hot and extremely hard—harder than any human penis she'd ever felt. It actually seemed to have a bone inside it like an actual dog's penis would have. The organ was short, but quite thick, with fat testicles. As she ran her fingers over his turgid flesh, she felt his scrotum heavy and warm on the back of her hand. Remembering Danni's instruction not to make the dog-teen come, she merely gripped the penis behind its head, doing her best to avoid the sticky spillage of pre-come that dripped in a wet trail from its tip to the floor.

Pet's tongue was dangling from the side of his mouth in his excitement. Heather tried to look sexy and enticing for the kid's benefit. Though in truth she felt like vomiting, she nonetheless maintained her alluring posture and squeezed her breasts with her free hand.

Then she heard a quiet click and next Danni said, "Alright, we're good to go. Let's get him in here with us!"

Heather let go of Pet's penis and Danni slid the cage door open. Pet quickly bounded inside the cage.

"Alright, get down on your back, doggie," Danni cooed through her white head mask. "Oh, I'm really gonna suck you off good now." While Pet lay down and rolled over, with his member sticking up and throbbing, Danni leaned in close to Heather and whispered, "Kiss the little piece of shit while I suck him off. Make sure he doesn't make a sound."

"Oh no! I'm not going to—"

Danni slipped her tee shirt mask off, revealing the horror that had been made of her face. "You want to wind up looking like me and be cooked here instead?"

Heather cringed on seeing the two deep and jagged triangular holes where Danni's pretty nose used to be. "Okay, okay, you got it."

She watched while Danni knelt over Pet's erection and took it into her mouth. She felt revolted when Danni went deep, deep throat on the penis. Then Danni twisted her head around on Pet's penis and stared at Heather, a look that clearly screamed, "Kiss the fucker! What the hell is wrong with you!"

So Heather did. She placed her mouth over Pet's and plugged his lips with her tongue. Pet was already twitching, his deformed body trembling in ecstasy as Danni sucked on his erection. He began kissing Heather back, while she did her utmost best not to vomit into his mouth. Then Heather remembered that she was supposed to strangle him to death and placed her hands firmly around his throat, ready to start squeezing once Danni gave her the signal.

Hey, what is the damned signal anyway? Heather realized that Danni hadn't told her.

But then she realized too that Danni hadn't needed to. Because less than a minute after Danni had begun sucking Pet off, Pet suddenly began thrashing violently like he was in intense agony. With her mouth pressed against his and her tongue blocking off his cries, Heather was first confused as to what was happening. But Pet kept thrashing. So Heather quickly replaced her mouth on his with a hand, and looked down his body.

She cringed at what she saw. Somehow, Danni had gotten Pet's balls into her mouth too and now she was biting Pet's entire genitalia off. Her jaws were clamped tight on the root of the penis, and with the way her lips were pulled back off her teeth as she strained at the fat piece of flesh between them, her braces made her teeth look like a chainsaw. The muscles in her neck were stiff and fat as gym-ropes. She'd already done a massive amount of damage to Pet; blood covered Danni's mouth and chin and more was squirting wildly everywhere.

Heather quickly moved her other hand also to cover Pet's mouth. She pressed his lips down as firmly as she could and also secured one of his flailing arms between her thighs. She hoped Danni would finish quick. She didn't want to take her hands off Pet's mouth and try to throttle him instead, but she wasn't sure how long she could keep him restrained and silent, particularly if he tried to bite her.

But both Danni and Pet were already done. Danni gave a huge wrench of her head and Pet's entire genital package came away between her teeth.

Pet gave a sudden almighty jerk of agony and went limp. It took Heather a few moments to realize that Pet was dead. And not just because Danni had castrated him, but because she'd also accidentally covered his nose along with his mouth and by so doing had smothered him.

Once she removed her hands from his face, Pet just stared deadly up with his mouth open and his tongue filling it like a purple gag.

Heather stared at Danni. Danni spat Pet's penis and testicles out and then grinned her almost-crazy grin again. "Well, I think I've had my ration of sausage and nuts for today." Danni was completely covered in blood now, and she made a show of rubbing Pet's blood into her breasts in a parody of how Electra Hemingway had coated herself in Maude's blood.

"Looks like the little mutant sonofabitch won't be having my nose and ears for breakfast after all," she told Heather with a gentle laugh. "Oh sorry, I forgot: *you* were supposed to kill him—I was just supposed to handle the fucking."

"I think we managed a fifty-fifty share in his death," Heather quipped back. Then a wave of nausea hit her and she bent over and threw up all over Pet's pathetic corpse.

"Hey, keep the goddamn noise down!" Danni whispered. "We still need to escape from this madhouse!"

CHAPTER 19

Getaway

"Which way?" Heather asked after they'd hurriedly gotten dressed. Danni pointed across the cave. "That farther tunnel."

"You sure?"

Danni nodded. "Yes. We can't exit the way we came in. Katie locked the trapdoor that leads up to the log cabin with another padlock, and I don't know where she put its key."

They were standing beside the dinner table with its spread remnants of the cannibals' recent grisly feast, and Danni pointed back towards the cage and giggled. "And I guess it's too late now to ask Katie's son where it is." She grinned at Heather again, her lips pressed tight against the fabric of the tee shirt that she'd once more wrapped around her face, though this time she'd not used the entire shirt; instead she'd cut away a wide strip from its rear with a knife and used that in 'stick-up-guy' style, hooking it on the stump of her nose and then running it beneath her eyes and under her ears and finally tying its ends behind her neck. "So we go the other way. Don't worry, Heather, *there is* an exit that way—remember when I asked where we were supposed to get water to do the dishes from, and Runt—or was it Katie?—told me we'd go fetch water from the river? So, that way leads to a river. And if they use it regularly, I don't think it's locked like the other one."

A slight smell of alcohol clung to both young women now, as they'd drank Katie's remaining wine and eaten some bread while getting dressed.

"Alright, let's go," Heather quickly agreed. While Danni was speaking, her gaze had moved over to the eternally bubbling stewpot. It was a reminder of the fate that awaited them too if Katie's family woke up now and found them. Particularly after what they'd done to

Pet. She didn't feel in the least bit sorry for killing Pet. The little piece of shit had deserved what he'd got. Killing Pet had actually felt good—like she was taking back some sort of control of her life. It was just unfortunate that it couldn't have been Runt's penis that Danni had bitten off. The way Heather felt now, she would have happily helped Danni bite one of its twin heads off. Alright, but not Six-Six's horrible phallus though; Heather didn't want that disgusting, fungus-covered penis anywhere near her mouth.

But wishful thinking aside, right now and directly in her line of sight, Danni's ears and nose were roasting on that skewer. And this was a dire warning. According to Danni, Katie and Runt had retired to the first of the cave's side rooms, while Electra and Six-Six where still in the middle room. Danni had also said she'd heard the mother and son having sex again, but that that had ended about an hour ago.

Physically, Heather felt refreshed after her short sleep, but she was wary of having to run anywhere. Her bitten right ankle seemed okay—as in it wasn't hampering her movements any—but she wouldn't trust it if she was fleeing at high speed.

"We need to arm ourselves," Danni whispered, walking over to the 'kitchen' table. There she picked up a long knife and shoved it down the waistband of her jeans, then began examining another in the flickering firelight. "Take your pick. We've a choice of knives and short spears, if you favor these skewers as weapons. Too bad the damn cannibals weren't drunk enough to leave one of their shotguns outside."

"Or their cellphones. Katie has one and Runt must have a cellphone too—that has to be how he kept in contact with her while they set their trap for us."

"Forget their phones," Danni said with a dismissive wave of her hand. "We're so high up in the mountains that we'd never get a signal."

Heather was glad that Danni seemed to have thought of everything. One of the first things her friend had done after they'd left the cage was to remove one of the rechargeable wall lamps from where it hung. The lamp now protruded from her left rear jeans pocket.

Then Danni caught sight of her roasting ears and nose and shook her head sadly. "Aw shit, but it's gonna cost a fortune in plastic surgery to make me look cute again—that crazy bitch went total Bibi Aisha on me. My parents are gonna freak when they get the medical bill for this." Then she grinned at Heather. "Hey, d'you feel like eating me?"

Heather gaped at her. "Huh? What the fuck are you yapping about?"

Danni's grin got broader, her braces pressing wetly against the tee shirt. "Oh, I don't mean in a lesbian way." She pointed to her skewered facial organs. "I mean, eat *those*. After all the trouble Katie went to—I think she even added salt and spices—it's a shame to let them go to waste."

"Hell the fuck no-o!" Heather realized that Danni was going to need major psychiatric counseling once they were safely away from this madhouse. She grabbed her by the arm and dragged her away from the stewpot and table. "Let's just frigging go before one of them wakes up to pee and finds Pet's corpse."

"Yeah," Danni easily agreed, "but take a knife too. They might come after us."

Heather nodded, took two steps back to the table and grabbed the first knife her fingers touched. "Alright, I'm armed. Now let's go find the river."

They set off for the cave's far exit, but then suddenly Danni pulled up again. "Hey, Heather, don't you wanna know what's been making that horrible smell?"

Heather wanted to yell at Danni to get a move on, but Danni was right: she was intrigued herself.

The stink that Danni meant, and which had to be coming from Katie's diseased and invalid father—the cannibal family's patriarch—was so unique that it demanded investigation. They were standing right beside the last of the cave's three doors, and here that nasty odor was right in their faces.

"If I don't see what's behind that door," Danni said, "I'm gonna wonder about it for the rest of my life. It's gonna haunt me like a ghost."

Heather understood exactly what her friend meant, but Danni explained anyway: "That smell . . . it doesn't smell like anything natural . . . not like anything in God's creation; there is something perversely evil about it. And I don't mean 'evil' like Katie and her insane teenaged mother and creepy brothers are evil. That's just deranged *human* evil. But the smell coming from behind that door . . . well, it's something else, something I can't find a name for . . . it's just . . ."

Heather nodded. "Okay, let's have a quick peek and then get out of here. It's dangerous to keep wasting time like this." Heather was agreeing because, just like Danni had said, if she didn't see what was responsible for that unholy reek, she knew the stink would haunt her, and given time, might even become the fuel for nightmares. God knew she was going to have nightmares aplenty if they survived this, but having nightmares about this smell too was something she definitely didn't need.

Silently, and with excruciating caution so as not to waken the sleeper behind the door, Heather turned the door handle and pushed it open.

Then, followed by Danni, she stepped inside to satisfy her curiosity about the room's occupant.

And then, both young women wished they'd never opened the door.

The thing in the room—which, by a process of elimination (since the room had no other entrances and there was no one else inside it) had to be Katie's 'father' and Electra Hemingway's 'husband'—looked like a giant pig with a human head and a body that was segmented like a worm's. This pig/worm body was a pale brown in color, completely hairless and ended in a long and scaly tail that looked like it belonged on a giant rat.

Worst of all, the thing was covered all over with a thick and transparent slime that visibly bubbled from its pores and dribbled down its sides to cover the floor; a floor on which lay rotted human remains. Heather stared hard. This impossible creature's slime was visibly evaporating, which meant it was responsible for that inexplicable and repellent stench, which, now that they were inside this room, seemed to have completely replaced the air.

The creature seemed to be sleeping. Its eyes were closed and its head lay on the floor between its front legs. It had a short fringe of black beard around its chin, but otherwise its head was as hairless as the rest of its body.

"Holy fuck!" was all Heather managed to get out. After that it felt as if her breath had frozen in her throat.

"Are you honestly telling me this is Katie's dad?" Danni asked, her muffled voice full of disbelief. "This *thing?* Now I understand why she's so fucked up. She can't help it—it's in her genes."

This short conversation had awakened it. As they stared at it in shock and horror and disgust, the pig-worm-human-monster thing opened its eyes and lifted its head to look at them; then a smile came over its human face and it opened its mouth and grinned broadly at them. Its eyes and teeth were as black as night, and its teeth were large and triangular.

It chortled on seeing them, a thick red tongue laving its lips hungrily. "Oh, fresh meat. How are you, fresh meat? Why not let my darling wife Electra cook you first?"

Then it pulled itself up from the floor and shambled towards them with its cloven hoofs splattering slime everywhere. It moved with hungry determination, but was almost as slow as a snail.

With Heather biting her hand to stifle the loud scream threatening to rip out of her throat, both girls turned and ran; both were almost out of their minds with fright.

Somehow, Heather just remembered to shut the door behind them.

"Oh my God, I didn't need to see that," Danni gasped. "I really didn't need to see that. Now I'm going to need therapy for sure!"

The monster's echoing laughter followed them all the way to the tunnel. "Come back, fresh meat! Come back to me! I want to eat you both!"

CHAPTER 20

A Gory Jory Discovery

On returning again to the clearing where he'd parked his Jeep, Hank paused beneath a sturdy oak to survey the area and make sure that Jory wasn't waiting to ambush him.

The aluminum sheet that Hank had buckled on underneath his hunting jacket felt uncomfortable in the summer night heat, but he didn't dare take it off. He was also beginning to sweat a bit and was considering taking a short break from his searches, wondering where he could nod off safely for a while that wasn't inside his ride.

He also itched for a cigarette, but he didn't dare light up in case either Jory or the monster (or both of them) saw the cigarette's red glow and smelt its smoke.

Yeah, one makes sacrifices to achieve one's aims. I won't die of nicotine deprivation if I lay off the Marlboros till this is all over.

Then suddenly he felt something wet dripping on his head.

He leapt back from that spot and then clicked on his flashlight and played its beam up into the oak tree.

"Aw shit, no!" he groaned on seeing Jory's disemboweled corpse dangling from the branch overhead. "Not again! Now I've got to start all over again."

CHAPTER 21

The Charnel Room

"What the hell was that thing?" Heather asked when they were about a minute's journey down the tunnel.

"Katie's dad, what else?" Danni replied her.

"You know that's *not* what I mean. We both saw it, and it spoke to us and . . ." Thankfully, the monster's smell had now faded again to manageable levels. In fact, the cold air blowing up the tunnel towards the cave had all but eliminated its abominable odor.

Danni stopped walking and pulled Heather to a standstill also. "What do you want me to tell you then?" Then she calmed down a little. "Hey, girlfriend, I don't know, okay? . . . Some sort of chemical mutant?"

"Or maybe a demon?"

Both young women were breathing hard and fast, a combination of their half-run down the tunnel and their fright. Heather was trying hard not to look at Danni, who looked really creepy in the shadow-light from the rechargeable lamp that they'd taken from the cave and which Danni had dimmed (by wrapping a napkin around it) till they had just sufficient illumination to see by, but not enough to give away their approach to any persons or creatures lurking ahead of them in the tunnel. Danni looked quite scary with that blood-splotched fabric masking half of her face, but she'd have looked completely ghoulish if she'd not masked herself up. And maybe it was due to adrenalin rush, but Danni seemed to have even forgotten how badly deformed she was; and Heather was sure that her wounds had to hurt like crazy. And with the way she was wheezing now, with the fabric sucking into the holes where her nose had been each time she drew in a breath . . .

On Heather's part, her ankle was holding out well so far.

Danni shrugged. "No, I don't think that that was a demon. I mean, I don't know for sure that it wasn't . . . but, do demons even exist? I'd prefer to think of it as some chemical-induced mutation or the results of intense redneck inbreeding—"

"Danni, it had a man's face and a pig's body and a fucking rat's tail, goddammit!"

Danni started them walking again, pulling Heather along after her, both of them holding their knives poised to stab whoever got in their way. "Okay, I'll accept whatever explanation you do; let's just keep moving before that freaky thing wakes up its cannibal family and tells them to chase after us." Then she paused again. "Hey, do you smell that?"

Heather stopped walking and nodded. "Yes, smells like rotten meat." Despite Danni's assurances to the contrary, she was now worried that they weren't actually headed towards the river.

Danni pointed. "The smell is coming from that opening."

The indicated opening was about ten yards ahead, an upright gap in the tunnel wall just before it made a sharp left turn, and from which light faintly spilled into the corridor.

They moved cautiously forward again. Heather would have preferred if they'd made a mad dash down the tunnel, but she understood Danni's caution. They had no idea what awaited them ahead and any error of judgment on their part could prove fatal. And besides, this opening might also lead outside. She doubted that it did though; with the tunnel obviously continuing beyond the opening, she had a gut feeling that this wasn't the exit they were seeking. Nor did Danni seem to think it was either; Heather sensed as much from her friend's body language.

As they stepped forward, the reek of rotting flesh seemed to thicken into a wall that threatened to block their passage to safety.

They reached the hole in the tunnel wall and peered inside, and instantly understood why it stank so bad.

"I think we've found the 'charnel room' that Katie kept mentioning yesterday," Heather said.

"Yeah," Danni agreed, making a retching sound.

The charnel room was full of corpses. It was another cave—about sixty feet across from its entrance to its far wall and about thirty feet wide. A wide crack in its far wall let in shafts of the rising daylight, so that they could see quite clearly in here, but a quick look around also showed them that this cave didn't lead outside the mountain.

From where both girls stood, the cave floor was level for two yards and then it sloped downwards and appeared to descend into a huge and very deep pit that extended across to the far wall. The girls got this impression of the pit's depth because, looking down between the top layers of the bones and rotting uneaten intestines that filled the charnel room, all they saw were more and more bones and rotting intestines, locked and webbed in a grisly tangle that might possibly descend forever into an intra-mountain abyss. Some of the skeletons belonged to children and even babies. The whole revolting mass swarmed with worms and maggots and blowflies.

A few yards from their feet lay a fresh red intestinal mess that Heather assumed were Maude's recently removed guts. The two green eyes peering desolately from the faceless skull of the fresh skeleton nearby (one that also had its crown sawn off) confirmed the remains as hers.

The smell in here wasn't something that the human mind had words for.

"How frigging old did Electra Hemingway say she was anyway?" Danni asked in horror.

"About three hundred and forty, I think. Why?"

"Because that's the only way that we're going to figure out how many bodies have been dumped here over the ages."

"If you accept that Electra is as old as she claims," Heather said in a trembling voice, while wondering exactly how much insanity she'd be able to cope with before needing a strait jacket and a nice comfortable padded cell, ". . . you'll also have to accept that that thing in that last room is a supernatural creature."

"There's nothing supernatural about these skeletons though; except if these maggots and flies everywhere are the confused souls of the dead. This is sheer wholesale murder. You're sure Electra's surname isn't Hitler? This looks worse than those Auschwitz photos."

"Insane. Insane."

They stood there staring, traumatized by the sheer extent of death on display. This pit of dead bodies represented more than just a mere disregard for human life, or a total lack of consideration for other people's right to exist. Rather, it spoke—no, screamed loud and clear—of an insane appetite, of a hunger that had lasted for possibly centuries and might go on forever; and one that would prove inexplicable to forensic psychologists.

Yes, there was transcendent evil here, evilness of a kind that Heather couldn't comprehend.

Danni though, managed to express it in simple terms: "Damn, you mean they actually *ate* all these people?" While saying this she was kicking a long tangle of rope and wood that lay just inside the cave entrance, and beside which stood an old oak table on which sat two plastic buckets, a rusty machete and another coil of rope. Behind the table stood three plastic drums like those near the fire in the upper cave. Heather now dully noted for the first time the rollers at the bases of the drums.

"That's some real demonic appetite," Danni said, giving the tangle of rope and wood one final kick.

"Uh huh, that seems to be about the sum of it," Heather agreed. The rope-wood thing that Danni was examining with her foot struck her as being familiar, but her thoughts weren't focused on it and as such she glossed over its immediate significance and that of all the other objects in the cave that weren't human remains. Her sole concern now was to not become another one of these unfortunates that Katie's mad family had filled their hell-pit with.

Finally, she shoved Danni out of the charnel room. "Let's get out of here while we're both still alive. We can't keep stopping on the way like this."

"Yeah, you're right," Danni agreed as they hurried on, "but something about that much murder just gets to me. Staring at that corpse pile back there, I felt so damn pointless and insignificant." She waved the knife she was holding at Heather. "I actually felt like slitting my own throat and lying down among them and just dying, draining away and becoming part of the great zero—fading into a human nothing. I think I know now how the Holocaust victims felt, all those poor innocents being herded like sheep into the Nazi gas chambers, knowing they were going to die and knowing too that there was nothing they could do to alter their fate in any way." She sighed deeply. "It was a horrible nauseating feeling, but also a compelling and very seductive one—like I'd just become the shit of the universe and would be doing the world a favor by flushing myself away."

"Danni, you're scaring me."

Danni began laughing crazily under her breath, which Heather found even more scary.

But thankfully, there was light at the end of their tunnel. Another two quick turns in the tunnel and they emerged from the mountainside into the dawn sky.

CHAPTER 22

The Mother of the Damned

Katie bent over Pet's bloodied body, her horror and pain spilling from her soul in a long and anguished low-pitched growl that conveyed more emotion than words could ever express.

For a long time she found herself unable to move from the spot. She sat on the floor, cradling her dead son's body and weeping profusely over it. His eyes were open and they stared at her as if asking the reason for his death by castration.

How could those two bitches do this to me!? How could they!? Her sorrow was so intense that it at first paralyzed her.

Katie had gotten up to urinate and then afterwards had come outside for a drink of water. It was then that she'd looked around for her deformed son and found . . . his corpse.

Katie finally got to her feet. She laid Pet down gently on the cage floor, shut his staring eyes for him and then left the cage. Wrapped in her cloak of grief, she'd hardly even noticed the film of vomit that covered him.

She walked with purposeful strides. It was clear which way the fugitive girls had headed. Down, not up—that intellectual idiot Danni was certain to have figured out which was the safe way to flee.

I'm gonna get them. And I'm gonna kill them both.

Katie didn't bother trying to wake her family. Six-Six was always impossible to rouse in the morning anyway, while Runt had drunk an entire additional bottle of wine before falling asleep last night and so would also not wake up. For her part, Electra couldn't run anywhere on those deformed toenails of hers, so Katie saw no point in asking her to join in the chase.

By Katie's watch it was right about dawn now.

She grabbed a long and glittering knife off the dinner table and headed down the tunnel that led to the river.

As she went, she sorrowed. Pet's death firmed a resolution that had been growing in Katie for almost a year now:

I need to leave this crazy family. I just have to—I gotta get away from these people for good before I go nuts!

***

Katie was almost going out of her mind from all the incest crap in her life. Her family's perversions went much further than just her giving birth to deformed twins—Pet and Toilet—courtesy of her impregnation by her father.

Take her two siblings, for instance. Although Six-Six and Runt were both brothers, Six-Six was actually Runt's son by Electra. And now Electra was apparently pregnant with Six-Six's baby too.

And Katie had just realized that she'd missed her own period again. And whose monstrosity would it be this time—Father's? Six-Six's? Or Runt's? No, it couldn't be Father's—those pregnancies only lasted nine hours.

The last 'child' that Katie had given birth to hadn't had a head—it had had five legs, one arm, and a foot-long wet tongue sticking out of its throat. It had been alive, but had gone into the stewpot nonetheless. She'd wept for days afterwards.

So now, once she'd killed these two bitches who'd killed Pet, she was leaving the cave on some pretext and not returning, heading west in her pickup truck all the way to Ohio, or maybe even farther away to Iowa or Nebraska. She knew she'd be safe over there; for obvious reasons, no one in her family ever traveled.

And whatever town she finally wound up in, she was having an abortion first chance she got. Electra could keep Toilet—she shuddered at her other child's demeaning name—at least the child wouldn't die of hunger.

Katie wouldn't miss the cannibal lifestyle. *Human meat does taste nice, but procuring it's so much trouble—I'm gonna stick to beef burgers like everyone else. And with Electra eternally hinting at someday telling us the secret of her eternal youth, but never actually sharing it . . . I think she just likes looking younger than me, younger than all of her children . . .*

Children. Katie had long ago accepted that her family was abnormal in more ways that one . . .

In addition to the nine-hour pregnancies that resulted whenever her father impregnated either Electra or herself—nine hours from conception to childbirth?—most of her parents' children were born deformed. All such were killed and eaten by everyone else to strengthen the family bond. Katie could count at least thirty of Electra's babies that this had happened to. And seven of her own as well.

Then there were all those other undeformed infants that Electra and Father (whose actual name was Boku Voss) had sacrificed in their blasphemous rites.

Every child in Katie's family also grew at alarming rates. The giant Six-Six, for instance, was actually just seven years old, but already fully grown—and he'd been like that since he was three years old. Katie didn't know if Six-Six's pronounced lack of intelligence was similar to Pet's (both of her twins *were* subnormal, and had been left alive merely on one of her mother's nasty whims) or if he was mentally challenged simply because his mind hadn't yet caught up with his body's age.

Her own life . . .

Katie and Runt had been raised by Ms. Shannon Gardner, a foster mother who lived in the small town of Washington, MA. Her parents had paid Ms. Gardner a lot of money—demon gold—for her silence, mainly because it had quickly become apparent that both kids were growing at alarming speeds. Katie and Runt had both been homeschooled, as that was the only way to conceal their abnormal growth rates. Once both children were in their late teens—which had taken about a third of the usual human growth time—Electra and Father had kidnapped and eaten Shannon Gardner.

And so both children had been inducted into the Hemingway family's cannibal way of life. Electra had wanted her normal-looking son and daughter educated so that the family would be able to survive in these modern times.

And they had survived. In fact, they'd even thrived.

***

But now . . .

Now Katie had had enough. Pet's murder had brought things to a head. Katie felt she was clear-sighted for the first time in her life. And since Electra seemed to have no intention of actually sharing the secret of eternal youth with her, she was getting out and not coming back.

Once she'd first killed Heather Forrest and Danni Melcher, of course.

Rage boiling over in her heart against her two sometime friends, Katie Hemingway hurried down the tunnel.

CHAPTER 23

Heather

Heather and Danni had emerged onto an isolated mountainside cliff. Dawn had just broken, the sun's light beaming a stately gray from the eastern horizon.

The river lay twenty feet below them, its gushing waters studded with rocks that turned it into a course of rapids at this point. Pine trees stood both near the cliff and across the river, and far off, below the tree-line, lay farmland green with summer crops. In the distance on their right rose several other mountain peaks.

Most important, there was no way down. The cliff edges dropped steeply to the riverbank. Nor did this cliff form a shelf that extended along the mountain wall; it was just a stone outcropping about six yards square. Staring up and across the mountainside to the right of where they stood, Heather made out the other cliff, the one with the house that led into the cannibal's cave.

"How do we get down?" she asked Danni. "For that matter, how do *they* get down?" She pointed down at the sparkling, foaming rapids. "This is clearly where the family get their water supply from, but how?"

Danni knelt and examined two sturdy metal spikes set in the cliff floor about a foot in from its edge. Then she looked up at Heather. "The rope ladder in the room with the corpses, this is what it's for."

"What rope ladder?"

"That rope-and-wood thing on the floor that I was examining. It's a rope ladder. It had two hoops at one end. I'm sure they'll fit comfortably around these spikes."

Heather sort-of remembered the thing that Danni was describing: it had been on the floor and she'd been kicking it. "Oh, so that's what it was? Alright, let's go get it."

They no longer needed the rechargeable lamp, so Danni now switched it off and placed it down on the cliff. Then they stepped back into the tunnel and hurried back to the charnel room.

Heather entered the corpse cave first and instantly turned right towards what they'd come for. She didn't want to look at that pit of dead people again. Remembering that all those people had been *eaten* (of all things!) threatened to unnerve her afresh.

She bent and picked up the rope ladder from its place on the floor. Then as she straightened up again, she went sprawling as Danni bumped into her from behind. While trying to keep her balance, Heather was forced to let go of the knife she'd been clasping in her left hand, and she heard it clatter away into the corpse pile. She finally steadied herself by grabbing the oak table which the ladder had been lying beside. To do this though, she first of all had to let go of the rope ladder, which was quite heavy, and she also wound up knocking the pair of buckets off of the table. The buckets' motions caused the rusty machete on the table to spin towards her. Heather jerked back quickly, just avoiding being hit in the nose by the machete's blade.

"Hey, watch where you're going!" she growled as she turned around. "You almost shoved me into the corp— . . . oh fuck, no!"

See, Danni was now back upright too, only not by her own power. Katie had a hold of her from behind with a hand clamped around her throat. Katie's other hand was twisting a long knife in Danni's lower back, the point of which emerged from Danni's belly. Danni's mouth was wide open behind her outlaw mask. She had a look of utter helplessness in her eyes, the knowledge that she was dying, that her life was over now no matter what she did. Blood was streaming from the hole in her belly. Her knife slipped from her fingers and clattered to the cave floor; Katie immediately kicked the knife backwards and out of sight.

"Stop it!" Heather took a step forward, but Katie pulled Danni back with her towards the cave entrance and before Heather could reach them, pulled her knife out of Danni's back and brutally slit her throat with it. She dug the blade deep into Danni's neck and as she pulled it across, jerked the other girl's head violently back with a handful of her brown hair, so that the severed musculature and windpipe opened up like an orifice and her neck vertebrae showed a sick white in the cut. She then tossed Danni sideways onto the corpse pile and left her to bleed out. As though a million bones were shattering all the way down to Hell, the pile crackled with the additional weight. Danni lay there with her hands gripping her neck, trying in vain to stop the fatal blood loss.

With Danni now as good as dead, Katie advanced on Heather with the knife raised and ready to stab her.

Heather retreated quickly. However, with Katie blocking off the cave entrance and with the corpse pile on her right (on her left stood the cave wall), she could only retreat the way she'd just advanced. Soon, she was stopped by the sturdy oak table that had held the buckets. The rope ladder almost tripped her up, but she managed to keep her balance.

"Stop! Why are you doing this to us!?" she howled.

To her surprise, her desperate question halted Katie's murderous advance. Katie paused, naked except for her denim cut-offs and streaked with Danni's blood. Not taking her eyes from Heather's, she licked the blood off her knife and smiled, her bloodlust apparently a little sated by the murder she'd just committed.

Heather, aware that she was now both unarmed and defenseless, tried to appeal to the sane side of Katie's mind, if there was one. "Katie, I asked why you're doing this?"

Katie smirked and gestured across at Danni's corpse. Danni was dead now, just another of her family's numberless victims. She grinned at Heather. The look in her eyes informed Heather that she felt sure of herself now, certain of their relationship as hunter and prey, and that it was merely a matter of time before Heather shared Danni's nasty fate. Katie's piercing blue and confident gaze also explained that as Heather's life was now *hers* to do with as she pleased, she could and *would* be magnanimous to her now and would stretch out these few remaining minutes of Heather's human existence like a rubber band, while also toying with her like a cat does with a mouse before eating it. This would be enjoyable psychic sadism.

"Just listen to yourself," Katie replied her question, lowering the knife to her side. "You sound just like the dead nerd over there."

Heather trembled with fear. "Whatever. Why are you doing all this?"

"That's the most idiotic question of all time. You two bitches killed my son. I'm more than justified in killing you both."

"Fuck you. You were going to kill us anyway. And *eat* us too, Hillbilly Sue. And I don't mean *that*, I fucking mean *this*!" Heather gestured sideways at the corpses. "How can anyone justify all this? You're eating babies too?"

Katie laughed. "Oh, that's Electra's doing. And anyway, some of those babies were *her* kids"—a wistful note of sadness now crept into her voice—"yeah, and mine too."

"WHAT THE HELL IS WRONG WITH YOU CRAZY PEOPLE!?" Heather couldn't restrain herself from screaming out the question.

Katie shrugged. "My mom's like a witch, see? And yeah, she really is as old as she claims to be, like three centuries and a half. Hey, Electra was there at the Salem witch trials. One of the many that got away unscathed. She always says she loves how history's being rewritten nowadays in the movies and media, with everyone saying that the witch trials were all about condemning innocent girls who'd had sex out of wedlock and all that other nonsense. Nah, mom says there was lots of actual witches in Salem, lots of covens in that general area. Only thing is, they were the smart ones—see, the real witches protected themselves by professing faith in God and joining in the witch hunt." She laughed. "Yeah, Electra and her coven, all of 'em guilty as sin, joined the hullabaloo and fingered the innocent and got *them* sentenced to death in their place. It was the easiest thing in the world."

"So why'd she flee then? I'd imagine Salem or Boston is much more comfortable that this cave in the wilderness."

Katie laughed again. "Oh, she got careless. See, after the Salem witch trials ended, mom and her coven—indeed most of the witches in that area—all pretended to be good churchgoing women. They all became the most respectable matrons and matriarchs in the North Shore region. Electra even married a preacher, the Right Reverend Isiah Hemingway, which is where we got our surname from—as our actual father Boku Voss doesn't have one.

"Witches make great wives, you know, what with all the sex magic and romance spells they do. I'm sure the good reverend had no idea what hit him once Electra got him into bed. And you've seen how damn pretty she is anyway. But soon Electra began getting old, and the ritual to renew her youth required her eating the flesh of a newborn child. She was past menopause by then, otherwise she could simply have gotten pregnant and asked one of her coven to midwife her delivery and claim the kid was stillborn. Long story short, she snatched a church deacon's newborn daughter and got seen doing it. So she fled before the law came for her.

"My real dad? Well you saw him on your way down here, didn't ya? Yeah, he's something from the pits of Hell. As for all the killing we do? It's a family necessity. Father loves the taste of human flesh and Electra provides it for him in abundance . . . and Runt and I, well we—"

While talking about her family, Katie had herself grown careless. Confident that she had Heather cornered, she'd let down her guard and was addressing her as if they were still friends. And Heather had suddenly realized that she wasn't as unarmed and defenseless as her initial state of fear had led her to believe. She'd realized that the machete lying on the table behind her was a deadly weapon.

"—Really like the taste of people too. Like dad says, we're not like you everyday folks. We're supernatural too to a degree and—"

With a loud shriek, Heather spun around towards the table, grabbed the machete and whirled back again with the machete lifted, its rusty blade traveling up through the air and down again as fast as she could move it.

"—So we're entitled to eat you lesser beings and—"

Katie never finished her sentence. Her eyes and mouth opened in surprise as Heather's machete slammed deep into the side of her neck, almost slicing her head off.

Katie made a stabbing motion with her knife, but she was too badly damaged to finish it and her fingers spread and let the knife clatter harmlessly away. Blood squirted from the left side of her neck as she stood there wobbling. Heather jerked the machete out of her neck and swung again. This second swing, with which she had intended to completely decapitate Katie, instead passed over the top of her adversary's head, because Katie collapsed to the floor right when she began swinging.

"I'm surprised that you look so surprised," Heather said as Katie bled out over the charnel room floor with a confused look in her eyes. "Yeah, you're actually dying, cannibal girl—deal with it."

Smirking when her ex-friend seemed to be pleading with her for mercy, Heather then chopped off Katie's head anyway. Then she kicked her severed head into the corpse pile. "So yes, I just killed you, bitch. Go hang out with the dead. Give Danni and Maude my sweet regards. Tell them I'm gonna miss them."

Then, keeping a firm hold on the bloody machete, Heather picked up the rope ladder also and carried it outside to the cliff. She hung the rope ladder on its spikes and descended the cliff face to the riverbank.

Shit! Danni's dead! she thought as her feet touched the green grass of freedom. *But I'm still alive and I intend to stay that way!*

Then, realizing that the river had to lead down the mountain, she ran off down the riverbank. She figured she'd reach civilization sooner or later.

CHAPTER 24

Bathroom & Toilet

On her way to using her bathroom that fateful morning, Electra Hemingway stopped for a moment to admire herself in her dresser mirror. This was something she did on most mornings, vanity being a by-product of perpetual unblemished youth.

Her reflection pleased her: her beautiful face, its youth maintained by dire sorceries; her eggshell-pale skin, creamy white and looking oh so delicate, like it would crack on the slightest tap; her perfect figure.

Good heavens, yes, I really do look eighteen years old!

Her long raven-black hair . . .

She waved a hand in front of the mirror and scowled. Not everything was perfect though. No matter what she did to tame her fingernails and toenails, they always grew out exactly the same, twisted and cracked and looking more like strips of dried corncob husk or tree bark than the attractive transparent tissue strips that nature intended them to be.

And doing something about them was itself a pain . . . Cutting her nails hurt as much as if they were a living part of her body, so as much as possible she left them untrimmed. One manicure and pedicure every two years was about as much as Electra could bear.

This single blemish is the price of my eternal life, she mused. *I just have to get used to it. It is difficult though, being so beautiful and yet still imperfect. So young and desirable and yet . . .* She looked over at her bed, where Six-Six lay snoring gently, and sighed. It helped that her lovers—her demon husband and children—thought her perfect anyway.

The urge to empty her bowels came again and Electra abandoned her appreciation of her looks and dashed into the bathroom.

One of the drawbacks of living this high up in the mountains was the lack of modern plumbing. Not that Electra knew what modern plumbing was; she'd never once been in a modern bathroom. Electra's bathroom was designed to eighteenth century standards, with its most prominent feature being a large wooden bathtub.

Her latrine was a potty. She sat on it and did her business, then got up and whistled sharply.

Shortly afterwards, her other grandchild poked its ugly head out of a hole in the bathroom's stone wall.

The only thing vaguely human about Toilet Hemingway was its head—though even this looked apelike. The rest of Toilet's body was wormlike, long and segmented and dripping slime like its father's body did. Now it slithered out of its hole and dropped onto the potty and began feeding.

Electra watched it with disgust. She couldn't stand the nasty thing, but there was no denying its usefulness.

She'd almost dropped it in the stewpot when it was born, but see, the pressure of childbirth had made Katie both shit and piss herself in her efforts to push her twins out, and no sooner had this horrid worm-thing been born than it had looped its segmented body around and begun feeding on the slimy turds between its mother's legs. By the time Pet had been born too, the little monstrosity was done cleaning up Katie's mess. And that was how Electra had named it 'Toilet,' a name that Katie utterly detested.

Needless to say, keeping alive this particular grandchild of hers (because it lacked sex organs, she'd never figured out if it was male or female) had paid huge dividends in the sanitary department. The family no longer had to walk down the tunnel to empty their feces over the cliff into the river.

Toilet was even more stupid than Pet though, and other than eat the family excrement, did nothing else but sleep in its hole in the bathroom wall.

Returning to her bedroom, Electra sat on her bed and took in the sweet smell coming from the main cave—that delicious odor of cooking meat. The taste of human flesh was something she lived for. And when there was fresh meat in the pot? Oh, wonderful. She licked her lips and in a frenzy of hungry anticipation raked Six-Six's back with her nails as he snored, drawing blood but not rousing the slumbering giant.

The clock on the wall gave the time as 6:30 a.m.

It's too early for breakfast now anyway.

Electra wondered whether to wake Six-Six up and make love to him again. She pressed her palm to her belly, trying to feel the baby he'd already impregnated her with. Then she looked towards her bathroom and saw Toilet slithering back up into its hole.

Her lips pursed in disgust. *Oh, I just hope this child I'm carrying now isn't another freak. How many children have I borne over the years and thrown into the stewpot because they were unviable life forms? Five hundred? Seven hundred? Ah, it's just so depressing.*

And then, suddenly her mind turned to the subject of the 'Gutter.'

It was a thorny problem. *How in Hell's fiery blazes do we trap it again?*

Electra really wished she'd never cast the spell that had summoned the Gutter to the human realm. *I can't even imagine the trouble that damn thing is causing in the outside world . . .*

The main problem in snaring the Gutter was its cunning. It wasn't particularly intelligent, but it had a deep instinct for self preservation. The Gutter could hold a human form for months and never alter that shape or break character except if it felt that there was danger to its person. Add to this trait a minor telepathic ability and the Gutter (oh, how Electra was beginning to hate that damn name!) was almost impossible to trace. Her demon husband had told her as much when the Gutter had fled their cave, and time had proven him right.

Well, I need to locate it and quickly at that and dispatch it back to Hell's Abyss. And next time I'll be much more careful when—

Her bedroom door opened then and Runt rushed in.

Electra instantly read the alarm in his eyes. "What is it, son?"

Runt gasped out the words: "Pet and Katie are both dead, and the girls . . . one of 'em's dead and the other one's escaped."

She trembled at his answer: *Escaped? Katie dead?* No one had ever escaped from them before. Nor had any outsider ever killed a member of her family before.

We Hemingways are the ones who do the killing, not the other way around.

An intense rage filled Electra Hemingway and she turned and began shaking Six-Six awake, raking his back brutally with her nails.

"You two boys be sure to catch that girl before she flees the forest," she ordered Runt in a cold voice while rousing the giant. "And remember, I want her *alive.*" She pointed to the cat-o'-nine-tails hanging on the wall and smiled cruelly. "When you bring her back here, I'm going to lash all the skin off of her!"

CHAPTER 25

Heather

Heather had been jogging along the riverbank for almost an hour now, following the river's curve as it flowed downhill. Although she knew she'd make better linear distance if she abandoned the river and just ran in a straight line, she also realized she'd quickly get lost if she did so; at the moment, the pines and other trees grew so high around her that she could hardly see the sky. And looking through the trees, the countryside she'd glimpsed from higher up seemed to have disappeared; squint all she liked, all that Heather saw ahead and below her now were the tops of other trees, and neighboring mountains above and beyond those.

Also, she found herself forced to make frequent stops in her flight. If she ran for too long, her right ankle starting hurting badly.

Heather was making one such stop now. Cursing Katie's dead son for subjecting her to this pain, she limped over to a tree and sat with her back against its trunk. She sighed in relief as she took the weight off her right foot. She laid her bloody machete by her side and examined her right ankle. It was purple and swollen, but she had no choice but to keep running on it.

She stared at the water flowing past just a few yards in front of her feet and worked to calm herself, tried to build up her mental strength for the next stage of her flight. She was well aware that the cannibal family must be awake by now and would be pursuing her down the mountain. A crystal clear memory of Danni lying dead amidst the charnel room's stripped corpses, with her throat cut ear-to-ear, filled Heather with terror for a moment, but she grimly forced the image out of her mind.

I am going to survive this, she told herself. *No matter what happens, I am going to survive this.*

She adjusted her legs in front of her and absently plucked a blade of grass and sniffed its morning freshness. *It's Runt that I really need to worry about. Six-Six is too stupid to be any use in a chase. But despite being so short, Runt is just as fast as Six-Six and his brains actually do work. So . . . yes, he's going to catch up with me soon.* Then she placed her fingers on her machete and smiled coldly. *And you know what? Maybe I'll wait for that deformed-penised jerk and let him find me . . . I remember Katie too thought she was invincible . . .*

Then, hearing a noise on her right, Heather gave a start and tried to pick up the machete. But a booted foot had already stomped the blade flat against the grass.

"Dammit, I'm caught again," she spat aloud.

But then she looked up at the person who'd stomped on her weapon and saw that it was neither Runt nor his mentally-challenged brother Six-Six. This man was older, middle-aged, and was more of the sort of man you'd expect to find working at your local bank or post office. He was unkempt for sure—unshaved and haggard-looking in dirty hunting clothes, muddy boots and a blue Red Sox baseball cap—and he was pointing a pump-action shotgun at her, but he didn't seem like he subsisted on a diet of human flesh.

She heaved a sigh of relief and said, "Thank God you found me, sir. I'm running from some crazy people who've killed my friends. Sir, do you have a cellphone? I need to call the police and report this."

Then the man smiled down at her and she had her first inkling that maybe she'd been wrong, that maybe he was crazy too, just a different, 'less insane' sort of crazy.

"Hi, miss," he said in a gruff voice. "My name is Hank Rollins and from this moment onward you work for me, alright?"

Heather nodded slowly, realizing that yes, this man *was* crazy. Still, she felt less worried. *But, okay, this is employment, not murder or cannibalism. Anything to get out of here, so long as he doesn't plan on killing or eating me.*

"I think I can handle that, sir," she said. "What's the job?"

He frowned. "I need your help in capturing a monster that's been prowling these woods and killing folks." He gestured over his shoulder, at a disemboweled male body that lay on the grass a short distance away from them and which Heather somehow hadn't noticed when she'd stopped here to rest. She figured it was either that the blood-splattered corpse had already been lying on the ground when she arrived here and she'd not noticed it because she'd been too winded to pay attention to her surroundings, or that Hank Rollins must have either dragged or carried the body here, though she'd not heard any sound of it being pulled along or dropped on the ground.

"That was my last assistant Jory," Hank explained. "The young fool wouldn't obey my simple instructions to stand still." He regarded Heather sternly, waving the shotgun at her to indicate that she rise to her feet. "Miss, for your own good, I sure hope you've got more sense than him."

Heather just gaped at her new captor. She couldn't find any words to say.

CHAPTER 26

Runt & Six-Six

"Sorry, sis, but you're food and we's all gotta eat," Six-Six quipped while licking his lips. "I'm sure you understand."

"Hey, cut that out," Runt said, cuffing his giant son/brother across the back of the neck. But he couldn't resist licking his own lips too. Katie looked really delicious hanging there like that. Yeah, really delicious. In fact, if they didn't need to begin their pursuit right away, Runt would have fetched his butcher knives and gotten right down to preparing Katie's headless corpse for the stewpot.

"Too much meat," Electra had grimaced when he and Six-Six had hauled in the bodies from the charnel room. "We'll have to smoke most of it or it'll spoil."

Runt agreed. He and Six-Six had hung the three bodies (Damn, they bit off Pet's cock too?) up on a row of steel hooks near the cave exit, near a spot where a constant draft of cold air came in through cracks in the cave wall. Keep 'em fresher for longer that way.

Electra was meanwhile pacing inside her bedroom, beside herself with rage. She was whipping everything in sight with her cat-o'-nine-tails—her dresser, the bed, the floor, the wall . . . Runt had tried to tell his mother to get a grip on herself, but then she'd tried to whip him too, so he'd split.

"Alright, let's go," Runt told Six-Six. "I already know where we'll find the runaway girl."

He led the way back down the exit tunnel, out onto the cliff and down the rope ladder.

"See, it's simple enough," he told Six-Six once they were both down beside the boisterous rapids. "She don't know where she is, so she's certain to follow the river downhill. But the river don't run straight, see?—so she's gonna be traveling in a curve that's almost thrice as long as necessary." He grinned an ugly grin and kicked a pebble into the rushing water. "While we, well, we're just gonna walk over to that clearing by the river where we found those two bodies two months ago and wait for her to show up there. We set out now, we'll be there in half an hour tops." He looked at the sun. "It should take Heather at least another hour to arrive there. Then we just collect her again and head back home."

"Yeah, you're right," Six-Six said as they set off through the forest, his massive chest stretching out his blue 'I ATE APRIL TAYLOR' tee shirt almost to ripping point. To be honest, Six-Six didn't understand a thing about the logic of the pursuit. He was just happy that there was lots of meat to eat at home now. And his next question was: "Hey, Runt, what's we gonna do for meat procurin' from the city now that Katie's dead?"

That question brought a bitter taste to Runt's mouth. "I dunno, li'l brother, I really dunno. But Electra's sure to think of somethin'. Just you leave it to her."

But a solution had already occurred to Six-Six: "How 'bout if we just let the Gutter kill people, then we pick up their remains? Just like we did with that woman and teenager it killed at the clearing we're headin' to?"

This suggestion made the muscular dwarf grimace like he'd tasted something rotten. "Li'l bro, I wish life were that simple."

CHAPTER 27

Heather & Hank

Heather, now bound to a sturdy riverbank sapling with rope and duct tape, sort-of understood what her captor had told her. How that crazy shapeshifting creature that she'd seen yesterday, right before that even crazier rain of shit had begun raining on she and her friends' girlie parade—the crazy thing that Katie's even crazier family (maybe the craziest family of all time) called the 'Gutter' because it fed on human guts—had killed Hank's family, and so, because he'd been devastated by his loss, now Hank was using her as human bait to trap it, because the original guy he'd kidnapped had escaped and gotten himself gutted.

Which made Hank crazy too. Which, considering how unkempt he looked, was easy to believe.

"Don't worry, I'm a fair shot," Hank had even had the nerve to tell her. "I'll definitely splatter it to bits before it tears into you. And, like I said, I'm employing you for this—I'm going to pay you afterwards. Ten grand."

Then he'd flashed an envelope of cash at her. As if that made any difference.

Heather felt maddened by the whole concept of being abducted and then being re-abducted. Who the hell did that ever happen to?

Hank was obsessed with angles and trajectories. Though he'd bound her securely to the tree, the bonds weren't really tight because he was still checking that he'd get a clear shot. She watched in dread as he backed away from her towards a tree with a high wall of grass around it, and then crouched out of sight in the grass. He'd seemed to magically vanish. She caught the flash of his shotgun barrel and then he reappeared again.

"No, no," he said, hurrying back across to her. "You're too far over to the left. I need you a bit more to the right; that way the beast has to come around to where I can get a clear shot at it." He reached her and began loosening the ropes around her legs.

"Listen, mister," she said nervously, addressing herself to the back of his Red Sox baseball cap because he'd bent over to see her ankles better, "those cannibals I told you about are coming after me. Waiting here really isn't a good idea."

Having freed her feet, he straightened up and laughed. "Cannibals, you say?"

"What, you don't believe me?" With her chin, she gestured up at the peaks across the river. "They're up there somewhere in the mountains, and I killed two of them and so they're certain to be pursuing me!"

He looked that way dismissively. Despite the bloodstains on her arms and clothes, it was obvious to her that he didn't believe a single word of what she'd told him of her ordeal. He was locked in his own mental world, intent on accomplishing his peculiar task.

"Yeah yeah, girlie, sure I believe you," he said. "I'll keep an eye out for them, okay?" He pointed back to where his shotgun stood propped against a tree. "I'll take care of your cannibals when they get here."

"Why won't you just call the police?"

Hank scowled at her. "Because the police couldn't help me the last time. Junior died right over there"—he pointed to the water's edge— "and he was gone when the cops arrived and they never found his corpse." She saw the start of tears in his eyes. "And so, I'm handling this myself and you're helping me and don't waste your spit trying to talk me out of doing what I've got to do here today. Besides, if I call the police, I'll need to explain about Jory and I'll be unable to do that."

"B-b-but—!" Then she shut up. She'd just remembered something: *Hey, hold on a minute. Didn't Katie's brothers say something about finding and carrying off two gutted corpses in these woods a few months ago—a middle-aged woman and her son? Were those Hank's murdered family that they ate?*

She considered mentioning this to Hank, but then decided that telling him would be an additional waste of time. He'd think she was mocking him. At the moment his mind seemed unable to accept any knowledge that might weaken his resolve.

So, if he won't listen to me, I desperately need to find a way to escape from him.

While Hank had been tying her up, Heather had noticed him appraising her face and figure. In particular his eyes kept going to her breasts, her tee shirt now plastered to them with sweat. He clearly found her attractive. She decided to try and seduce him. If his wife had recently died, he'd definitely not had sex for a while.

"Okay, okay, I'll go along with it," she said with a coy smile. "I'll help you catch the monster willingly. Just tell me what to do and I'll do it."

He eyed her suspiciously. "You will? No more trying to escape?"

"Yes I will, but I want to be paid first."

"You got it." Hank pulled the cash-filled envelope out of his jacket and stuffed it into her left front jeans pocket. "That better?"

She nodded. "Uh huh. But there's one more thing."

"What's that?"

"Hey, can we like . . . make love first?"

"Huh?" He gaped at her. "What?"

She nodded. "Yes, let's make love. Lovemaking relaxes me and with all this kidnapping and re-kidnapping happening to me, I'm so tense right now that I feel like screaming." She looked at him expectantly, concealing the anger she felt towards him. The question was, would he bite the bait? She watched his eyes and saw that he was seriously considering her request.

Then he shook his head. "Well, girlie, this is neither the proper time nor place for sex. Oh yes, I do think you're very pretty . . . but, how about if we do it *after* the creature's been caught, huh? Then it'll be more like a celebration."

She just restrained herself from shrieking at him, though her voice still came out very loud and irritated: "Because you might fucking miss hitting your monster and hit me instead. Or it just might kill both of us, which means I'll still be dead." She had tears in her eyes now and they weren't entirely from playacting. Breathing slowly and deeply, she calmed herself. "So please, fuck me now, while we're still alive and have the chance to do so."

"Hmm," Hank said. "Well, when you put it like that, I really can't refuse your request." He placed a hand across her lips. "Just don't shout again—you might scare the damn thing away."

She didn't realize she'd been that loud. "Yeah, sure," she whispered, relieved that he'd begun untying her. Then she grinned seductively at him. "Just free me, baby. I can't wait to suck on your hard cock."

While he hurried to untie her, she made her plans to escape him. She was glad that she'd read him right—he'd been lonely for so long after his wife's passing that her offer of sex had seemed too good for him to pass up. She knew she was quite attractive, and clearly her ordeal of the past twelve or so hours hadn't lessened her physical comeliness.

Or maybe, he just likes the disheveled way I look. We are in the wilderness after all. The big question now is—should I try to bite his dick off while giving him a blowjob, or make him hump me extra-hard and then hurry over and pick up his shotgun once he falls asleep?

She was certain that Hank would fall asleep after having sex with her. He'd been yawning since he'd abducted her. He didn't seem to have slept all night.

However, she opted for the first option. It seemed nastier and thus a more fitting and more satisfactory payback for this discomfort he was subjecting her to. *I'll suck him really hard, and then, right when he's about to come, I'll crush his balls with my fists and bite down on his dick and then I'll run across and get the shotgun. And then I'm gone from here!*

Hank had just finished cutting her free of the last of the duct tape. Quickly, before he could attempt to kiss or undress her, Heather dropped down on her knees and began undoing his belt.

She was surprised to find the metal plate strapped over his belly.

"Hey, man, what's this for?" she asked, tapping on it with her fingernails.

"Is it in the way? I'll just take it off," he replied distractedly and then quickly slipped off both his hunting jacket and the aluminum plate belted around his middle. The plate made a musical clang when it struck a rock a few feet away.

Wow, he really did come prepared for the monster, Heather thought, pulling Hank's pants and boxer shorts down to his knees (intentionally, so that he'd not be able to run after her when she split). Then she popped his already stiff penis in her mouth and began sucking on it. Hank's penis was much cleaner than Runt's had been. It was just a little sweaty though, as if he'd not bathed for a day or two.

"Oh yeah, honey," Hank said, resting his hands on her head and running his fingers through her hair. "Oh, baby, you've no idea how long it's been since . . ."

Heather sucked doggedly on his penis. She sucked deeply on his hard length. She took his testicles in her hands and fondled them firmly. She wanted to be ready to crush them when he ejaculated, and if it had really been as long as she suspected since Hank had last come, then he wasn't going to last long now.

But then she heard the sound of someone approaching. Footsteps walking on grass.

Her first terrified thought was that Runt and Six-Six had found her. *Am I about to be abducted for the third time? Oh God, but that would be too cruel.*

"Don't stop, honey!" Hank groaned when she slipped her mouth off his penis to see who was approaching them. She was ready to dash off into the woods but Hank had a firm grip on her hair and wasn't letting go.

Heather looked to her right and gasped. She saw herself—*Hey, that's me!*—walking out of the woods towards them. The approaching reproduction of herself was perfect in every detail, even down to the bloodstains she'd gotten on herself while killing Katie.

"Hey, what's going on?" But Hank had seen what she had too. He stared at the approaching Heather, then he looked down at the Heather who'd been fellating him and then back up again at the one walking towards them. Clothing and otherwise, both girls were completely indistinguishable from each other.

"Hello, mister, I'm lost. Do you know the way out of these woods?" The voice was exactly Heather's too, as were the girl's mannerisms, her warm smile and the way she leaned her head slightly to the right.

Hank, his fly open and his penis still stiff, just kept staring as the young woman got closer.

Heather, however, had already realized what was going on. In a flash she'd recalled the man who'd changed shape into a monster yesterday before dashing across the highway, and she'd also remembered Katie's family's comments about the 'Gutter' while they'd been holding her captive, about how the creature was a shapeshifter.

149

So she understood that this version of herself approaching them was actually the Gutter in disguise.

While Hank kept gaping in confusion, Heather ducked behind him and then shoved him hard towards 'herself.'

Unable to steady himself, Hank stumbled forward and met the other Heather. Then, wrapped in her welcoming embrace, they both fell to the forest floor. Hank's Red Sox baseball cap went flying off his head and startled a purple butterfly perched on a daisy.

Then Heather's doppelganger altered shape to something that was a mixture of snake and monkey and demon, and it dug its head and claws deep into Hank's belly and began excavating him like he was a pit. It tore his innards out of him in a red stream and chewed and slobbered wetly on them as if they were delicious.

Hank began screaming in pain.

Heather began screaming in terror.

CHAPTER 28

Runt & Six-Six

Alerted by the screaming, the two cannibal brothers burst out into the clearing a short while later.

Six-Six instantly hurried over and grabbed hold of Heather. "I bet you're glad to see us again now, ain't ya, baby? And Electra's just dyin' to see you again!"

Heather just kept staring at the dead man. Runt walked over to him and stared too. "Yeah, the damn Gutter was here alright. Shit, when the hell are we ever gonna catch that god-damned thing?" He turned to Heather and demanded, "Which way did it go?"

"Into the woods over there," the trembling girl replied, then she pointed down at the dead man. "He-he-he was raping me . . . wh-wh-when it c-c-came out a-a-and . . ."

Runt stared in the direction that she'd indicated. He peered amongst the trees and squinted for a while and then finally shook his head and waved his shotgun at his giant brother. "It'll be long gone by now—we'll have to come back some other time to hunt it down. Then he looked down at the dead man and grinned at his open fly. "At least you died with a smile on your face, buddy." Then a flicker of memory came to the dwarf's mind. "Hey, I know this guy! Six-Six, ain't this the fellow whose wife and son got killed by the Gutter right here and then we ate 'em?"

The giant nodded and gave an imbecilic laugh. "Hahahahahaha! Sure looks like him. An' now we'se gonna eat him too. What a delicious family they are!"

Runt, however, had just noticed something else. "Hey, what's that over there in the trees?" Before Six-Six could reply, he'd strode off to their left. He was gone between the tree trunks and thick green leaves for about thirty seconds, then he returned dragging another disemboweled corpse after him by its ankle, this body a young man's. The boy's empty belly looked like a mud pit somehow superimposed onto his dirty blue shirt.

"Hey, hey, just look what I found," Runt said with a disbelieving laugh. "The damn Gutter sure has been having itself a belly-timber party, ain't it?"

Six-Six laughed. "More meat for the pot, yessir. Hey, Runt, see what I'se saying 'bout letting the Gutter do our huntin' for us?"

Runt nodded reflectively. "Yeah yeah, kid, you just may be right 'bout that. Anyhow, we'll see what Electra thinks of your idea." He pointed his shotgun at Heather. "I'll take care of her, you bring up the two bodies. Can't leave good meat lying around to spoil." Then, ignoring Heather's impassioned pleadings, he picked her up and slung her over his shoulder in a fireman's carry.

Following Runt's lead, the giant Six-Six hefted one corpse over his left shoulder and the other over his right one.

Then, while Heather wept on the dwarf's broad back and pummeled it with her fists, the brothers started back up the mountainside.

It never occurred to either of the two young cannibals that they'd re-captured the wrong 'woman.'

CHAPTER 29

Ten Minutes Ago . . . & Now

Ten minutes ago . . .

While pushing her way through the trees in a fresh attempt to escape the forest, Heather had tried to fit her mind around what she'd just witnessed. As she'd shoved leaves and low branches out of her way, she'd replayed the events through her mind in disbelief.

How is that even possible? Yes, yes, I saw that shapeshifting Gutter creature yesterday, but this time it was me. IT WAS ME . . . ME!

Seeing 'herself' had been a truly surreal experience. And then, when her doppelganger had transformed into that 'thing' and begun ripping Hank apart, Heather had felt like reality was once more unraveling around her. She'd been unable to stop herself screaming. Her terror had felt like a physical thing that needed to leave her body or else it would drive her insane. She'd felt tranquilized, incapable of flight, unable to do anything except watch the monster tear Hank up and howl at the sight of his gory demise.

But then she'd realized that her screams would have alerted her cannibal pursuers to her presence nearby. So she'd ducked into the forest and begun hurrying away.

While making her way to freedom, Heather had felt rather sorry for shoving Hank at the monster. She'd now understood that he'd just been a miserable but determined man who'd wanted revenge on the beast that had eaten his family.

But really, I had no choice in the matter. And anyway, it was his fault that I was there in the first place.

Which had reminded her: *That $10,000 is still on me.* She'd felt her left trouser pocket to confirm this. *Yes, Hank was right; I certainly earned this money.*

It was then that she'd burst out into the clearing and discovered Hank's parked Jeep Cherokee.

Heather had felt like weeping when she'd seen the vehicle. Here was her escape! And more importantly, a pair of slightly muddy ruts extending from the Jeep's rear tires and leading back along the forest floor clearly showed the way that Hank had driven in.

Oh thank you, God. Now I can go home.

She'd walked over to the Jeep Cherokee and discovered it was locked. She'd stood there in the heat of the morning sun with her forehead pressed against the driver's window and pondered what to do. The dashboard clock was off, but the sun wasn't fully overhead yet, so it couldn't be noon yet.

The keys have to be on Hank. I'll have to go get them.

It was either walk back to the riverbank clearing and rifle through Hank's pockets for his car keys, or try to walk out of the woods on foot. And not knowing where she was, who knew how long that would take? The keys, however, were certain to be in Hank's jacket, which he'd dropped beside the tree she'd been tied to when she'd begun fellating him.

Besides, fleeing in the Jeep meant that she'd automatically be able to outrun the cannibals. And once she hit the highway, the only thing she was stopping for was a State Police cruiser. She'd weep for joy when the cops pulled her over for breaking the speed limit.

Which state am I in anyway? Massachusetts? New York? Vermont? Connecticut? Oh, that doesn't matter. I just need to get those car keys.

She'd had no weapon with which to ward off the 'Gutter,' but she was desperate. And desperate people did desperate things. Heather had understood that this was an all-or-nothing situation for her. *If I don't get those keys I don't have just the cannibals to worry about now—the Gutter might come after me too. In fact, it might be stalking me right now.*

That thought had almost started Heather running off through the forest anyway. But she was a brave girl. And if she'd learnt anything in the past twenty-four hours, it was her capacity to defeat the odds, to survive.

So she'd picked up a large branch off the forest floor and made her stealthy way back towards the riverbank again.

She'd been halfway there when she'd seen Runt walking quickly through the trees towards her.

She'd frozen on sighting the dwarf and had almost turned and run away. But then she'd realized that he'd not even noticed her. He was after Jory's corpse, which lay off to one side.

So she'd ducked behind a tree and waited. Whistling to himself, Runt had grabbed Jory by the heel and dragged him out of the woods. The dwarf was making so much noise that Heather hadn't worried about him hearing her as she'd followed him back to the riverside, where she'd hid behind another tree to observe what was going on.

Once again, she'd felt as if her world was coming apart at the seams. There 'she' was again, standing and looking scared, while the giant Six-Six covered her with his shotgun.

What sort of a crazy monster is this? she'd wondered in horror. *It looks EXACTLY like me and it's even acting and TALKING like me. Dad's always telling me to stop cocking my head to the right like that!*

She'd also been confused as to why the Gutter wasn't transforming and attacking the two Hemingway brothers. And as to why it allowed Runt to pick it up and sling it over his shoulder in a fireman's carry and bear it off. Her doppelganger hung across the dwarf's broad shoulder like some terrified ordinary girl, weeping and beating Runt's back in protest, while the giant Six-Six slung both Jory and Hank across his own shoulders.

What's this? she'd wondered *A protective mechanism that only makes it react when it feels it can win the conflict? Or is it just afraid of their shotguns?*

But that hadn't really mattered to Heather. What *had* mattered was that the brothers were now leaving, heading back up the mountainside to their damned cave of terror.

***

And now . . .

Heather sagged with relief as Runt and Six-Six vanished between the summer-green forest foliage.

Oh my God—I've made it! I've actually made it! I'm free! I've really escaped them!

Even after Runt's and Six-Six's voices had faded, Heather didn't dare move for almost twenty minutes. She stayed pressed against her tree until she was certain there was no chance of their returning.

It was only when she stepped out of hiding that she saw Hank's shotgun propped against the tree's front, concealed by the tall grasses.

So all this while I didn't have to hide from those two jerks. I could have simply killed them both.

Feeling some regret, she picked up the shotgun. She almost felt like starting off after Runt and Six-Six, hunting them through the trees, just like they'd hunted her.

But then she shook her head. *No,* she thought wisely, *it's actually much better this way.*

Shotgun in hand, she bent over Hank's hunting jacket and quickly found his car keys. Then, after a final glance up the mountainside that made her shudder with revulsion at all that she'd recently experienced, Heather walked back to the black Jeep Cherokee, climbed into it and drove off out of the woods.

Once she'd hit the highway, Hank's GPS reliably informed her that she was on Massachusetts State Route 43, by the New York State border. Smiling grimly, Heather quickly connected with Route 7 and sped south towards the city of Pittsfield to tell the police the tale of her ordeal.

It may take a while to make them believe me, but I'm bringing them back to arrest Electra Hemingway and her entire cannibal family. Danni and Maude deserve that much at least. All the cops need to do to locate the cave is follow the river like I did.

What the police would make of the family's mutant patriarch—the pig-worm-human hybrid in that last room, Heather didn't have the slightest clue.

But since she'd be the one leading them up to the cave, she figured she'd get to see the looks on their faces when they found Katie's father.

She grinned. That would be just priceless.

Suddenly feeling lighthearted, Heather turned on the car radio and looked for some music. Slain Jane's *The Other Side of the Rainbow* came on:

"Sometimes I win,
Sometimes I lose.
Sometimes I'm the predator,
But most times I'm just food . . ."

Scowling, Heather turned the radio off and just drove. Screw that imagery.

CHAPTER 30

Electra & . . .

Electra Hemingway glared furiously at the terrified 'young woman' that her sons had brought home with them. She lashed out her hand and struck the girl's cheek. 'Heather' went down in a heap on the cave floor.

"Please!" Heather gasped. "I'm sorry."

Electra spat down on her. "You're sorry? Pick her up, Six-Six, and turn her to face the meat hooks."

The giant complied. Heather was lifted into the air and turned to face the far end of the cave, where Katie's headless corpse hung beside Danni and Pet's bodies. Runt was just hanging up the two fresh bodies on the meat hooks too.

"So you're *sorry*," Electra said. "You're *sorry*. Is that all you can say after murdering my daughter and grandchild?"

"Girl, you ain't nowhere near as sorry as you're gonna be," Runt said, walking back past them to get himself a drink of water from the dining table. While there, he also indulged himself in some leftover human kidney from last night's dinner.

"How dare you kill them!?" thundered Electra. "How dare you murder my darling Katie and Pet!?"

Six-Six meanwhile, noticed Heather's scared glances at the worktable, on top of which Katie's severed head now lay, her mouth and eyes still gaping open like when she died.

"Don't'cha worry yerself 'bout that," the giant said with a goofy grin. "The head's there 'cos Electra loves eating brains—you don't want her to eat yours, do ya?"

Heather squirmed in his grasp. The giant had a firm grip on her right breast and was squeezing it hard.

"Put her down, Six-Six, and stop fondling her—there'll be sufficient time for that later. Runt, stop stuffing your damn belly and come tie the little hellcat to the whipping post."

The 'whipping post' was simply one of the sixteen wooden pillars that held the cave's roof-support beams in place. Two wooden arms extended from halfway up the pillar to the traverse—these were used for securing those due for punishment.

Heather was quickly undressed and secured to the whipping post, with her wrists tied to its wooden arms.

"Please, don't!" she whimpered in fright as Electra approached her with her cat-o'-nine-tails in her hand.

"You're lucky we already have five bodies to cook, or else it would be straight into the stewpot with you," Electra informed her with a cold smile. "But I'll teach you a lesson alright, you little bitch. After I'm done whipping all the skin off your back, I'll have Runt hamstring you so you can't run off again, and then I'll let Six-Six have you as his sex toy until we eat our way through all this meat . . ."

"Yeah yeah yeah," Six-Six said, rubbing his hands with glee and then grabbing his crotch, which was already swelling with anticipation. "Thanks, Electra!" Then the giant leered at Heather. "Yeah, gonna fuck your asshole with my cock, baby. Gonna fuck your asshole till its insides are all hangin' outside of ya! Looks like a pretty red flower like that. Yeah!"

Heather looked speechless, but not for long. Once the whipping began, she began screaming.

Heather screamed with each lash of the whip. But Electra quickly became aware that something was wrong. True, the young woman was howling in pain, but she clearly wasn't in as much agony as she should be. This cat-o'-nine-tails had bits of glass tied in its knots; with the way it was shredding Heather's skin she should have been shrieking the cave walls down as blood spurted everywhere as the whip tore her bare back to shreds.

And that was the other thing: This girl wasn't bleeding at all. What was emerging from her flayed back was some kind of black jelly.

"Boys, boys!" Electra hollered at her sons in sudden delight. "This isn't the runaway girl that you brought back! It's the Gutter! Hahaha! We've caught it at last!"

"What? The Gutter?" Runt paused in chewing his mouthful of human kidney and stared in surprise at the naked brunette girl tied to the whipping post. "That's actually the damn Gutter?"

Electra couldn't control her joy: "Yes yes yes, it is!"

"The . . ." Six-Six walked over for a closer look. "Sure looks like Heather to me, momma."

Electra rolled her eyes. *Oh, ye damnable gods of Hell's flaming pits, how could I ever have given birth to such an idiot?* Her mind began working fast. *Now that I've gotten it trapped, it'll be easy to dispatch the thing back to the Abyss I summoned it from.*

But the Gutter wasn't to be taken that easily. It was already slipping its shackles and changing form back to its deadly self. In a few seconds it was free of the whipping post. It crouched on the floor—a shriveled and hairless brown monkey-thing with a snake's head and claws like gleaming black scythes—and hissed at Electra, its mouth opening to show her its teeth; its single red eye shining with malevolence.

Oh no! Electra thought. *I made a huge mistake in letting it know that I'd detected its deceit. I should have kept my excitement to myself!*

But by then the Gutter was already leaping towards her with its claws poised to strike.

The Gutter hit Electra Hemingway like a barrage of bullets. She felt a sudden intense agony in her belly as if she'd swallowed a whole carton of razor blades. This overwhelming pain was followed by an equally intense feeling of emptiness. Looking down, Electra saw that most of her intestines were hanging out of her belly through a hole in her dressing gown, draped down over her groin, with some of their tangled coils reaching to her knees.

Howling in pain, she fell to the floor.

The Gutter stared down at Electra. It swiped its bloodied razor-sharp claws at her and she raised her hands to protect her face.

But then Six-Six yelled something and the creature was in motion again. Electra watched it leap out of the way of the knife in her giant son's hand and then hang suspended on the whipping post, exactly like a monkey would do. With herself out of commission, the demon-creature seemed to be making up its mind on who to attack next.

Runt was nearer so it went for him. The dwarf was still bringing up the shotgun to fire when the Gutter hit him full in the face, with both its hand and foot claws flailing everywhere. Runt and the Gutter both let out loud screams—one scream signifying an attack frenzy, the other intense pain. The shotgun went off and then fell out of Runt's hands.

Then the Gutter somersaulted over Runt and landed right-side-up on the dinner table, from where it scanned the cave while strips of red skin hung from its jaws.

Electra gasped. Runt stood there with his face ripped to shreds. His right eye was a mushy red pit, the other eyeball hung down his cheek on its nerve cord. His left cheek was torn open to reveal his teeth. In addition to this, the Gutter's foot-claws had ripped through the straps of his overall, so that it was slowly sliding down his body. Large parts of his chest had been peeled bare, with the torn-off skin and muscle floating like red flower petals over his exposed breastbone and ribs. Runt was clawing the air and moaning from a mouth with no lips.

"Shit!" Six-Six said, taking a step forward to go help his brother.

But either Runt was now deaf as well as blind, or he was so enraged or unhinged by his agony that he misunderstood the sounds he heard and thought it was the Gutter he was hearing, because as Six-Six walked towards him, Runt blindly grabbed a knife off the dining table and charged at him with it.

Confused, Six-Six got out of the way and clubbed Runt on the back as he shambled past him. It was a light tap, one merely intended to knock his older brother to the floor, but it was right at that point that Runt's overalls (which had been falling lower and lower since the Gutter had severed their shoulder straps) . . . it was right at that point that the falling overalls tangled up his ankles and tripped him headlong. And this meant that, under the combination of his own violent forward momentum and his brother's downward push, Runt went skidding along the floor towards the cooking fire.

"Look out!" Electra screamed, unaware that her elder son was completely blind now and couldn't heed her warning.

Six-Six tried to grab Runt's legs, but Runt had already gone past him. Flat on the floor now, Runt ended up under the stewpot tripod, with his head and torso deep inside the fire.

Now he really began screaming as his head and shoulders began roasting.

"Shit!" Keeping a wary eye on the Gutter, which was watching these happenings with an amused smirk on its snakelike face while licking blood from its claws, Six-Six hurried over and tried to pull Runt out of the fire. But he quickly realized it was useless. He couldn't see clearly through the flames, but Runt was tightly wedged down there in the cooking pit, impossible to shift without lifting the entire bubbling cauldron of meat off of its tripod. Runt was still screaming and kicking wildly and now his underpants were on fire and the smell of his burning body had mingled with that of the cooking meat in the pot.

Actually the whole thing smelt delicious to Six-Six, but he decided to try and move the stewpot anyway. But . . .

"Look out, son!" Electra screamed again. "The Gutter's right behind you!"

The giant Six-Six might have been slow-witted, but he had damningly quick reflexes. He spun around, saw the Gutter leaping at him with all twenty claws extended, and dived sideways. He didn't look back even when he heard the noise of the monster's claws loudly striking the side of the cooking pot. Instead he scrambled forward across the floor on his hands and knees and grabbed up the pump-action shotgun that Runt had dropped.

"Look out, son!" Electra screamed a third time. "It's almost on top of you!"

Six-Six rolled over and chambered a round. The Gutter leapt towards him again, its body bright red with blood, Electra's blood and Runt's blood. Its claws flashed at him like Death's welcoming angels.

Feeling as if his bowels would empty from fear, Six-Six pulled the trigger. The shotgun discharge blew the Gutter's head clean off its shoulders. The blast also flung its body back against the dining table.

Six-Six leapt to his feet. Chambering another round, he hurried over to where the monster lay. He shuddered as he stared at it—once again feeling that intense dread. Even though it now had no head, the creature's four limbs were all in frantic motion, fiercely clutching and clawing at the air, desperate to inflict hurt. Keeping well out of range of those razor-sharp claws, Six-Six shot the Gutter three more times, literally blowing the thing to pieces.

Then he put down the shotgun and hurried over to attend to his wounded mother. Runt was already dead from a combination of burning and smoke inhalation. His flailing legs had stopped their kicking while Six-Six had been battling the Gutter.

***

"I'm not long for this world now, darling," Electra Hemingway said weakly. "But before I die, I need you to do a few things for me."

Six-Six nodded with tears running down his cheeks. "Oh, Electra, don't leave me alone. What'm I gonna do without you?"

She pointed weakly towards the third door. "Your daddy—Boku Voss—he'll look after you."

Six-Six looked at his father's door and shook his head. He was really weeping now. "No, no, no—it ain't the same thing, momma."

Electra nodded sadly. "Try to be strong, darling. Things will be fine after I'm gone. You've a lot of meat to cook. Just remember to smoke the excess and never to mix together the raw and the cooked. . . . And . . . and later on you'll catch people in the forest below, and one of them will make you a good wife and also be a fertile mother to you and your daddy's children."

More tears and a scared look on the giant's face. "Noooo . . . noo!"

"Yes, darling. I'm sorry, but that's the way it has to be." Electra smiled calmly. "But for now, please do exactly as I ask, exactly what I tell you to. Will you do that, darling?"

He nodded.

"Good. Now carefully place of all my intestines back inside my belly."

Six-Six did so. "Er, Electra, how 'bout if I get a needle and some thread and stitch you right up again? Won't that help?"

"I've lost too much blood, dear. At most, I've twenty minutes of life left—let's just enjoy that together, okay?" She raised her head and gestured towards her bedroom. "Now, go to my dresser. Open the top drawer, there's a little black prayer book in there; bring it to me, darling."

Six-Six lumbered off through the door and quickly found the book and brought it back to her.

"Alright, honey," she said, taking the little volume from him. "Now, hold on for a short time while I leaf through this and find the right death prayers."

"Uh . . ."

"Be strong, my child. Be strong for us both." Blood spilling from her lips as she did so, Electra smiled sweetly at him.

Six-Six nodded. With tears streaming down his cheeks, he watched her study her little black book.

Her belly burnt with agony. Death was very close now—she could feel its ethereal touch, the relentless approach of her disconnection from this human realm of living beings and her translation through its timeless portal to the realm of shadows. Time wasn't on her side.

"Alright, I'm ready, darling," she told Six-Six, lightly stroking his cheek with her crooked fingernails. "Don't weep for me," she moaned in pain, then she shut her eyes and began a silent chant.

Six-Six wept anyway. He couldn't stop himself.

"Kiss me, kiss me, darling," she murmured. "Kiss your mommy goodbye."

He kissed her eyelids tenderly, and she resumed her chanting.

He couldn't stop himself crying as he watched her, his tears spattering her breasts. Oh, he was really going to miss her . . .

At least he got that much through his dimwitted mind. The smell of Runt's roasting flesh wafting over from the fire was distracting him. Maybe he'd eat Runt's dick for lunch. Six-Six wondered what that two-headed penis would taste like with garlic and tomatoes . . .

He began weeping again. "Oh, don't die, Electra!"

But then Electra's eyes snapped open and she smiled at him. Only now her eyes were like bubbling pits of tar, huge and black and liquid. And her teeth had suddenly lengthened as well into sharp spikes.

Six-Six felt a deep surge of dread. He had the sudden idea that he'd been tricked, but was clueless as to how. Bent over Electra's body as she lay there on the floor in her pool of blood, he felt scared for his life, more scared even than when he'd been facing off against the Gutter.

"What's wrong, Electra?" he asked in fear. "Why's your eyes look all funny like? And your teeth too?"

"Oh, darling!" she gasped. "You're so good to your dying mother. Mommy loves you!"

And then suddenly Six-Six felt an immense pain tear through his belly. Then the pain was deep inside his chest as well and going even deeper, like it was entering into his soul too.

"YEOOOWWW!" he howled. He first pushed himself up on his elbows to see better, then up onto his palms.

Oh, my God? Electra Hemingway had shoved both of her hands deep up inside his body. Her forearms were buried elbow-deep in holes punched through his "I ATE APRIL TAYLOR" tee shirt and his skin—holes from which blood now gushed down into her own ripped-open belly—and he could feel her hands working painfully in his chest.

"Wha . . . what . . . ? Electra, what are . . . ?" he gasped helplessly at her, then fell silent as she ripped his heart out of his body.

Six-Six gave his mother one last confused imbecilic look and then collapsed dead on top of her.

Electra didn't have the energy yet to shove him off. She ate his heart while he lay there on her.

Eating Six-Six's heart restored her, as she'd known it would. By the time she'd finished eating the juicy red morsel and had rolled her giant son's body off of her own, Electra Hemingway looked as good as new, unscarred and unblemished.

The only drawback to the healing spell was that she'd grown another two inches of thorny fingernail and toenail. But she guessed that couldn't be helped.

She got to her feet and, after a regretful glance down at Six-Six's corpse, surveyed the damage to her home.

She winced at the scenes of carnage in the cave: Runt roasting like a midsummer barbeque under the stewpot and the remains of the damn Gutter . . . splattered under her dining table like some grotesque bug that had hit God's windshield.

Well, at least we got YOU at last!

Staring at the Gutter's remains reminded Electra of someone else: Heather, the girl who'd escaped. Where was she now? Was she still hiding out in the woods, or had she gotten away?

By now, the little murdering bitch is most likely babbling her tale to the authorities.

Electra laughed softly. *But no matter, I've a way to fix that . . . To fix it really well.*

CHAPTER 31

Heather

Heather was in the Pittsfield Police Station.

She stared at the young policeman in disbelief.

"This is crazy," she said. "All of a sudden, I don't remember a thing that happened to me."

"What *do* you remember?" he asked cautiously.

Heather tried to stir up her memories but failed: "I just know that yesterday evening my three friends and I set out from Raynham to visit Danni's ex-boyfriend Ray up in Searsburg in Vermont . . . and . . . and after that everything is suddenly a blank until I walked in here a short while ago."

She looked around the room, perplexed even as to what town she was currently in. "I don't even recall how I got here or where I'm coming from . . . and why am I all covered in blood like this? Hey, what the hell happened to me?"

CHAPTER 32

Electra

Electra watched Heather's ghostly image, which was framed in a green cloud of smoke that floated over her outstretched left palm. Heather's confusion as she sat there in the Pittsfield Police Station was obvious, her expression quickly turning angry as she desperately tried to access her missing memories.

Electra laughed. *Oh, you silly, silly, silly little girl, you won't remember a thing that happened to you here in my cave. Not a thing . . . and not ever. The past eighteen hours have been erased from your mind for good.*

Once satisfied that her desire had been accomplished, Electra blew the cloud of green smoke off her palm. This 'erasure spell' was a minor one, but one that had often proved very useful; usually when spelunkers stumbled on the cabin above. Nowadays, Misery Mountain was swarming with people peeking into every damn crevice, and regretfully, one couldn't eat *everyone* one encountered—some folks were very important, it was better to let them leave alive than have the Massachusetts state government grow curious about their disappearance and begin investigating her mountain hideaway.

Electra *had* set up a stronger magical shield that masked the log cabin and the exit cave near the riverbank from inquisitive eyes (else her cannibal family would have been found out long ago) but sometimes a person with a strong psychic aura could see through it.

Frowning, Electra got up from her seat at the dinner table.

The cave was a mess now. It needed a cleaning which she wasn't yet able to attend to.

She peeked under the dining table. As a rule, an incarnated spirit couldn't remain in the human realms once its host body was too badly damaged to house it. To incarnate a demon in the human realm, the summoning spell must of necessity give it a material form that obeyed

166

Earth's physical laws. If that form was destroyed, or rendered incapable of supporting life . . .

Electra sighed. The splattered mess that had been the Gutter had already crumpled to black ash, but that ash still had to be swept up and dumped in the charnel room.

Also, Six-Six's body had to be hung up on the far wall with the others. And Runt needed to be cut up and put into the stewpot.

I'll handle all that later in the day. But first . . .

But first she had to go see her husband.

Even after two-hundred-plus years of marriage to Boku Voss, visiting that final room still filled Electra Hemingway with a mixture of excitement and horror. She understood that because of Voss's nature it would be impossible for her to ever feel differently—she was a demon's bride after all.

She pushed the third door open and stepped inside, reveling in the heady, terrifying odor that greeted her, an odor that had already made itself part of her own flesh through their intense and regular intimacy.

Boku Voss—porcine and gross and as inhuman as the pits of hellish darkness he'd originated in—waited for her in his bed of slime. On seeing her, a broad smile came over the demon's human face.

She walked over and sat beside him on the floor, letting his slime coat her naked body. She placed her arms around his neck, pulled his face close. Weeping, she kissed his fat lips.

"All of our children are dead," she informed him ". . . except for Toilet my grandchild."

Boku Voss laughed. "Yes, I too have sensed that. And now that they are dead we will have much meat to eat for months to come."

She wept, he laughed. After awhile he licked the tears from her eyes with his rough tongue, tapped her right thigh with a cloven hoof and asked in a gentle voice: "Darling, you are not pleased about this. What do you desire of me?"

"Three more children to replace the dead ones," she replied and then moved to kneel in front of him like a supplicant. "Three strong children—pure in your blood."

Boku Voss sniffed her belly. "But you are pregnant now," he said.

"The child is your great-grandchild. I offer it to you as a sacrifice."

That said, Electra lay on her back in front of her demonic husband and parted her legs for his pleasure. She shut her eyes and spread her thighs wide with her hands, gasping in pain when his tongue entered her. She screamed when the two-month-old fetus detached from the walls of her womb, hearing the child's similar psychic shriek of protest as it realized that now it would never be born.

Then the fetus was sucked out of her body and she heard her husband chewing and then swallowing it. She opened her eyes. Boku Voss was licking the fetal blood from his chin. She could feel the blood of her abortion leaking from her vagina.

"All your children are delicious," he told her.

"But that one wouldn't have grown up fast enough. Come, darling, let us start again. In three days I'll have borne three children for you. And in three months from now they'll all be strong and fast and deadly enough to hunt in the woods and catch more human prey for us to feast on."

Boku Voss nodded. "I love the sound of what you say. Yes, darling, let us start again. Come to me, my nasty human lover."

She moved under him. He dragged his porcine bulk over her until she was drenched in his unholy slime. And then his sex entered hers and she felt the immense satisfaction of knowing that things would soon be perfect again in her cannibal world.

The End.

ABOUT THE AUTHOR

Wol-vriey is Nigerian, and quite tall.

He believes there actually are things that go bump in the night.

He writes horror fiction—for adults only, please. And also some surrealist stuff.

Wol-vriey blogs at: *http://oddityfarm.wordpress.com*

WOL-VRIEY
BIZARRO AND TRANSGRESSIVE FICTION

BOSTON POSH (BUD MALONE #1)

In 2028 AD, the USA is a nation ravaged by hungry dragons and dinosaurs. In Boston, Massachusetts, private eye Bud Malone is hired to rescue a kidnapped heiress. But nothing is as it seems.

Malone works to unravel a tangled web involving Boston Chinatown, a 200-year-old woman with a 9-year-old body, white robots, a human-liver-eating psychopath, a golem, a porcelain dragon, and a snake goddess with a crush on him. There's also a woman obsessed with chicken sex. Then Malone meets Posh Lane, a gorgeous call girl who's desperate to quit her pimp.

Romantic sparks ignite between Posh and Malone, but Posh's past suddenly catches up with her in a BIG way. To save Posh, Malone agrees to run a quest for Earth's new rulers, the Forks. But, Malone has no idea that agreeing to the Fork's odd request will send him on the weirdest trip he's ever been on in his life.

BOSTON CORPSE (BUD MALONE #2)

MAGIC CAN BE MURDER! - Drag queen Lucy Tang is back in Boston, and is hell-bent on settling her vindetta against casino owner Sookie Ling. And suddenly, Bud Malone, PI, has the case of his life to resolve.

When Boston's robot police force are baffled by a mind transfer case, they come to Malone for help. The one person who can likely help Malone out here is the witch Soledad Bathory. But Soledad seems to know a lot more than she's telling him. It's a case not made easier when Malone meets Soledad's beautiful cousin, Josephine 'Slave' Bailey. Slave has her own plans for Malone, most of which involve teaching him BDSM and making him her new Master.

Oh, and Rick Rogers owes Sookie Ling a whole lot of money, a gambling debt that's going to be literally Hell to pay!

BOSTON CORPSE - Not your average detective novel!

Burning Bulb
PUBLISHING

WOL-VRIEY
BIZARRO AND TRANSGRESSIVE FICTION

BOSTON LUST (BUD MALONE #3)

"Bless it, Father, for she has sinned."

Seven murdered gay women, all their bodies completely drained of blood. All also with large parts of their bodies dissolved away like acid has been pumped into their veins.

Bud Malone has to find the female vampire preying on Boston's lesbian population.

Then Malone meets the beautiful Trudi Carmen and the case gets even more tangled. Trudi needs Malone's help in recovering a ring that's gone missing. But how in the world is one little black ring related to either the dead women or their killer?

Resolving this case will lead Malone deep into Lucy Tang's legacy—The Abstracta. And then to the city of Genesis.

Boston Lust—Just when you thought Bean Town was safe to visit again.

HELL DANCER

Six people find themselves trapped in Detention, a nightmare realm where the demonic Schoolmaster is hell-bent on reforming them . . . until they die.

Porn superstar Venus Deluxe came to Springfield, MA to party, and next found her life hanging by a thread. One wrong answer will mean her death.

Suspended BPD detective Tanya Rockford was trying to stop one kind of violence, but found a terrifying another. With her and her companion's lives hanging in the balance, it's going to take all of her courage and resourcefulness to escape this hell she's stumbled into.

Porn stud Chad Cannon has made a career from his ten-inch penis. Here in Detention, however, it's his brains that matter. He'll soon be hoping all the pot he's smoked over the years hasn't completely messed up his memory.

The three students, Sherri, Jordan, and Mike? They were all just in the wrong place at the right time. Will anyone survive Detention? The evil Schoolmaster doesn't plan on letting that happen . . .

Burning Bulb
PUBLISHING

WOL-VRIEY
BIZARRO AND TRANSGRESSIVE FICTION

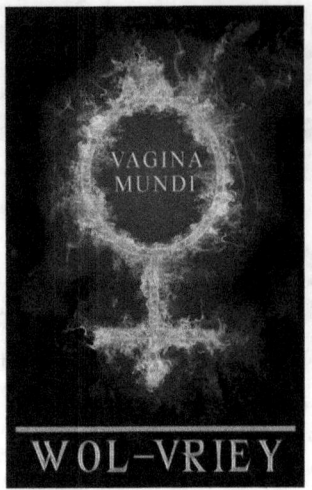

VAGINA MUNDI

Rachel Risk is a professional thief with super-strong hair that can stretch like tentacles to manipulate objects. Ashley Status has both a digitally augmented brain, and 'muscle-purses' in her arms and legs in which she stores inflatable objects—cars, guns, rocket launchers, etc.

When Raye is framed as the fall girl in a jewel robbery, the pair flee Chicago's vengeful robot gangsters and take refuge in the Hotel Bizarre, where the gorgeous 'vagina singer,' Femina, is performing for a week.

But the Hotel Bizarre is even stranger than its name suggests, and very soon Raye and Ash are involved in an deadly adventure, a struggle for survival the likes of which they'd never imagined possible—with loads of deviant sex, drugs, music, and violence at every turn. And just what is the old woman in the skin desert really doing with all those cats glued to her walls?

VAGINA MUNDI—a Bizarro Hymn in praise of WOMAN!

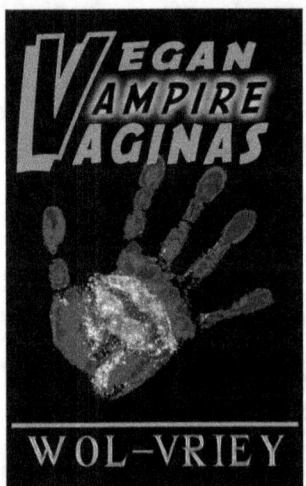

VEGAN VAMPIRE VAGINAS

The biggest bank heist in US history. And Tom Palmer can't remember pulling it off. And no, this isn't your standard case of amnesia. After a one-night-stand gone horribly wrong, Boston salesman Tom Palmer wakes up with a vagina implanted in his left hand. Then his day gets worse.

Tom is transported across space-time to a nightmare version of Boston, one where the Bizarro virus has transformed half the population into cannibals. Worst of all, Tom discovers that in this new Boston, he's the infamous gangster Pussypalm, wanted for robbing the Federal Reserve Bank of Boston a year ago. He also learns that the vagina in his hand is prophetic, i.e. it talks . . . after sex.

With 130 people left dead during his bank heist and six billion dollars missing, Tom knows he's living on borrowed time. It is in his best interests not to remember anything. Because once he does . . .

Burning Bulb
PUBLISHING

WOL-VRIEY
BIZARRO AND TRANSGRESSIVE FICTION

VEGAN ZOMBIE APOCALYPSE

In the post-apocalypse worlderness, zombies rule the earth. They're allergic to meat, and brains literally make them explode. Zombies now eat blood potatoes, parasitic tubers grown in the flesh of humancows corralled in maximum security farms. Two fugitives meet in the ancient ruins of Texas. The first is Soil 15-f, a womancow who's escaped her farm a week before she's due to be killed and her blood potato crop harvested. The second fugitive is Able Kane, former head necros food technician, now sentenced to death for heresy. But Soil is no ordinary humancow.

Unknown to herself, she's the vegan zombie agricultural revolution, and the zombies desperately want her back. And the necros equally desperately want Able Kane dead. He's fled with a forbidden discovery which will reshape the world for the worse if used. And Able is just hardheaded/misguided enough to use it.

MELANIE NEMESIS CATCHPOLE

In Springfield, Massachusetts, Melanie Catchpole is hired to fetch back a magic teddy bear worth millions of dollars from a warehouse across town. Problem is, the warehouse is down in Springfield's O-Zone—that totally weird sector of the city where Bizarro fell to Earth. The 'O' is a fairytale land, a place where dreams and nightmares literally live and breathe..

Worse still, the gingers—mutant cannibals—prowl the O. The gingers have already eaten everyone else Melanie's employers sent to get back the magic teddy bear.

Accompanied by the handsome but ruthless Doug Fisher (who she finds sexy but doesn't dare entrust her heart to), Melanie enters the O-Zone. Melanie and Doug are instantly caught up in an adventure they'd never have believed credible even if written as fiction . . . and Melanie's used to experiencing the very weird as the norm.

And now, additionally, there's a mystery to unravel: What does the dark, freezing-cold being called The Fixer want with Mary, the barkeep's daughter?

Burning Bulb
PUBLISHING

WOL-VRIEY
BIZARRO AND TRANSGRESSIVE FICTION

BIG TROUBLE IN LITTLE ASS

From Bizarro master storyteller Wol-vriey comes a truly weird western tale that will leave you awe-struck and on the edge of your seat...

In the town named Little Ass, tight-assed prostitute Rosa overhears a gunslinger's plans to assassinate rancher Edison Bennett. Once the badass Bennett learns of the plot, he ensures there'll be hell to pay for any attempt on his life!

Yes, it's going to take all of gunslinger Jude's shooting prowess, his eclectic collection of strange firearms, a trusty horse that requires an owners' manual, and the help of the lovely and invigorating Nell (who's EXTREMELY odd when the going gets weird), to survive the Bizarro hell that Edison Bennett unleashes in order to hold onto the land that he'd stolen from Madam Zizi.

BIZARRO 101 (A BASIC PRIMER)

Welcome to the strange place:

A collection of 37 flash fiction stories designed to introduce one to the Bizarro/New Weird Genre.

Weird, dreamy, nightmarish, absurd, sad, surreal, humorous . . . this collection of tales is all this and more.

***

"This primer is the very essence of any and all styles and types of Bizarro writing. Wol-vriey collects, distills, and bottles up these 37 tiny stories for your sensory enjoyment. This is an absolute must-read for anyone new to the genre, because it demonstrates the scope of what Bizarro is, and what it can be."
    –Teresa Pollack, Bizarro commentator and blogger

Burning Bulb
PUBLISHING

WOL-VRIEY
BIZARRO AND TRANSGRESSIVE FICTION

Dr. Orgasm

Courtney Taylor is young, intelligent, beautiful, and successful. She also has a boyfriend who loves her deeply. The problem is, no matter what Courtney does, she can't climax during sex.

When Florence Rigid's communist forces destroy the city of Metaphor, Courtney and her friends Teresa, Highball, Miki, and Heather are cast into the midst of a quest to find the only person able to save the land of Innuendo—Dr. Carol Orgasm, wanted by the communists for developing the O-Pill, a wonder drug that grants women sexual ecstasy on demand.

The communists will do anything to get their hands on the O-Pill and prevent its reaching the millions of Innuendo's women. But Courtney desperately wants that pill too. And so it's now a race between Courtney and the communists to find Dr. Orgasm first.

And Courtney has no choice but to win this race. She must win it: For her own orgasm . . . and for the freedom of female sexuality everywhere.

PUSSY TRANSMISSION

Pussy Transmission were the most decadent Pop Art ensemble of the 90's. Led by the beautiful painter Isis Lynch, the trio revolutionized the art world. Then suddenly, without explanation, Pussy Transmission vanished into historical obscurity. Now, twenty years later, three women come to Lynch Place. Lily and Nina are journalists desperate to interview Isis Lynch. Raven, on the other hand, wants to find her boyfriend, who's gone missing inside Isis's house. Raven's worried—she's heard that Pussy Transmission broke up because Isis began dabbling in black magic . . . with devastating results. All three women will shortly wish they'd never left home. Particularly once the rats in Lynch Place start warning them that they're going to die . . . and Raven meets Betty Butcher, the bouncy supernatural psycho who's intent on chopping her into bits. Pussy Transmission, Baby! Just because . . .

Burning Bulb
PUBLISHING

WOL-VRIEY
BIZARRO AND TRANSGRESSIVE FICTION

GIRLS ARE NOT SMILING

Welcome To The Road Trip From Hell

Pagan is demon-possessed.

Lori is suicidal.

Britt is just terminally pissed off.

Meet three young Boston women on the run from the law, each with problems that will fuse into more than the sum of their individual parts, becoming a holocaust of sex and violence and terror, a literal rain of blood and horror and gore and evil.

And if that wasn't already bad enough, Pagan's pet demon is slowly transforming her into something both unspeakable and unholy. Truly, these girls aren't smiling.

BLUE NIGHTMARES

Consummate EVIL is coming. It is relentless and unavoidable. It is Blue.

Jessica Schreiber is seeing things. Very horrible things. Since arriving in Raynham for what should have been a relaxing vacation, she's been seeing *The Big Blue*.

Jessica is smelling things too—dead and rotting things that she can't see. She is sure those dead and rotting things are dead people. Lots of dead people.

Jessica's worst nightmares will soon become her reality. Her reality will soon become a terrifying nightmare.

The tentacled residents of the House of Death have a lot that they wish to show Jessica Schreiber. They have a lot that they wish to tell her. But will she survive long enough to learn their lessons?

Burning Bulb
PUBLISHING

WOL-VRIEY
BIZARRO AND TRANSGRESSIVE FICTION

BRAINCHEW

It was supposed to be a simple jewel heist, but it went badly wrong. Chuck got shot and died.

Lance hid his friend's corpse in the Pleasant Street Cemetery. But that was a big mistake—there was something undead, something extremely hungry . . . something eXXXtremely horrible, buried in the Pleasant Street Cemetery.

And Lance had just woken it up.

They called the monster Brainchew because it ate brains. Human brains. And it preferred those brains fresh from the heads . . . of the living.

And now it was awake again, Brainchew planned on feeding big-time tonight. Oh hell yes, it did.

BRAINCHEW 2: OUT OF THEIR HEADS

After Tiff Hooper recognizes Josh Penham, the man who abducted her and kept her in his basement and abused her, she brings her three friends to Raynham for a night of well-deserved revenge on him.

Only things don't go according to plan.

It is never a good idea to leave a corpse in Raynham's Pleasant Street Cemetery. You run the very real risk of awakening what lies underground there. And that thing—Brainchew—is more horrible and more evil than anything the average mind conceives of even in its worst nightmares.

Brainchew is back! And this time the monster is extra-hungry. But there are plenty of delicious human brains about tonight, and Brainchew intends to eat them all before dawn.

Burning Bulb
PUBLISHING

WOL-VRIEY
BIZARRO AND TRANSGRESSIVE FICTION

DARIA: AN EROTIC NIGHTMARE

Even the best laid women can go wrong.

Daria Simpson is HUNGRY. She's HUNGRY for sex and bloodshed and death.

Shelly Parker just wanted to have a threesome with her boyfriend Craig and her best friend Erica. Everything was shaping up nicely for their weekend of sexual fun and games, until they stopped at the creepy Crossway Diner and met Daria.

From the moment they met Daria, EVERYTHING went wrong for them; and it went wrong in the most horrific and terrifying of ways!

Daria: Paranormal service has been resumed.

WET BONES

Greg is about learning the hard way that you don't mess with Aunt Grace.

Nine completely fleshless skeletons recovered in the Massachusetts woods. Two detectives on the trail of a horrible, hungry monster.

Broken-hearted Allie Jackson has a date with a creature from Hell.

Things are about to get well out of hand for everyone, and in horrifying, terrifying ways they don't expect.

Burning Bulb
PUBLISHING

WOL-VRIEY
BIZARRO AND TRANSGRESSIVE FICTION

MR. UGLY

When a rotting corpse appears and starts butchering Raynham's youths, there's really only one question that needs answering:

Is this faceless and rotting monster Peter Howard, or isn't it?

Problem is, Peter Howard died 15 years ago. So how can he possibly be back from the dead and murdering people with such relentless and incredible brutality?

Peter's mother Malicia, who's just been released from the lunatic asylum may have the answers to the crazy puzzle, but the two detectives investigating the deaths don't even know the right questions to ask her yet.

BRUTAL

Jane Winters is 28 years old.

She works as a checkout cashier in a department store. She's an attractive woman with a winning personality. She has both a photographic memory and an I.Q. of 189.

She's met the man of her dreams.

But she's also a cannibal with a unique and very scary mode of operation.

The group known as TULIP (The Urban Legend Investigation People) are out to either prove or disprove the legend of Insane Jane.

But have TULIP bitten off more than they can chew?

Burning Bulb
PUBLISHING

WOL-VRIEY
BIZARRO AND TRANSGRESSIVE FICTION

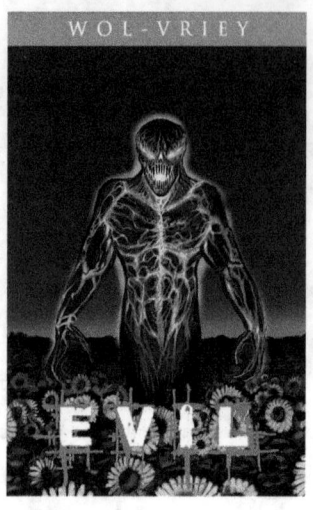

EVIL

The Evil began the week before Sylvia Stewart's 30th birthday.

Cathy Higgins died.

The Bargainer resurrected Cathy . . . for a price.

The price? Cathy's father Ronan had to plant some seeds for him.

But these were no ordinary seeds the Bargainer gave to Ronan Higgins. These were seeds from Hell: seeds which required human flesh as both soil and fertilizer.

And meanwhile, the unsuspecting Sylvia Stewart went ahead with the plans for her birthday party, which was to be held on Ronan Higgins' sunflower farm . . .

666

Ohio's State Route 666 stretches 14.7 miles between Zanesville and Dresden.

Most days, it's just a normal road with a funny name.

But for six minutes on the 6th of June each year, Route 666 becomes a gateway to somewhere else . . . a gateway to Hell.

Each year 13 unfortunates get trapped in the 666 underworld, with no way to get back home.

This year though, things are going to be very different. For one thing, there are currently a whole lot of turbulent human emotions at play in the underworld. And also . . . the psycho Al Gore is just about completing his collection of human heads.

And . . . what the hell is a church doing in Hell, of all places?

Burning Bulb
PUBLISHING

WOL-VRIEY

BIZARRO AND TRANSGRESSIVE FICTION

THE CLEAVERMAN

It began as a joke, a gag to pass the time that turned deadly. One rainy August night in Raynham, MA, nine friends jokingly invoke the evil phantom butcher called the Cleaverman.

These nine friends get a whole lot more than they ever bargained for. Because there's only one way to return the deadly Cleaverman back to the darkness he came from, and that is to solve his riddle, which starts: "Tell me the name of John Cleaverman's wife . . ."

And human beings being what we are, even with the Cleaverman out to butcher them all, our nine friends still manage to stir A WHOLE LOT of human misbehavior into the deadly mix.

At the rate they're going, it'll be a wonder if anyone survives THE CLEAVERMAN at all.

PERVERSE

When 21-year-old Heather Forrest accompanies three of her friends on a weekend trip up to Vermont, she has no idea what she's getting into.

Because, during a brief stop in the western Massachusetts woods, the girls get kidnapped and things go rapidly downhill from there. Soon Heather and her friends are fighting for their lives, fighting to survive the most perverted and impossible situation imaginable. And meanwhile, Hank Rollins is also in the woods, hunting the unholy monster that killed his wife and son . . . and he's hunting it with live human bait.

Oh yes, there will be blood. And there will be terror and buckets of gore also. And truly horrible atrocities will happen. Most definitely so.